COWBOYS & MOONLIGHT

A STARLIGHT SWEET ROMANCE

JACQUELINE WINTERS

Editor: Bridge to Story

Copy Editor: Write Girl Editing Services

Cover Design: Brennylou Designs

Proofreading: FictionEdit.com

CHAPTER 1

 bbie

There was nothing Abbie Bennington hated more than a rodeo.

Bright red signs rocked from wires strung over the street, taunting her. A promise that the thing she hated most would invade her town this weekend.

"Some luck, huh, boy?" She and her dog, Gibbs, strolled along the sidewalk to the *Starlight Gazette* office. The dog sniffed at a barrel filled with purple impatiens, indifferent to the disruption to an otherwise quiet week.

It'd been years since the big rodeo came to Starlight. Any rodeo, for that matter. The arena on the edge of town had grown over with weeds, its painted sign worn away to near invisible, wooden bleachers broken in places from various storms. It was a forgotten relic until earlier this summer when a new investor snatched up the property and a happy realtor finally pulled up its long-present *For Sale* sign.

She did a double-take outside the storefront window of Bennington Tack and Saddlery, her parents' store, where a large, full-color advertisement for the rodeo was taped to the inside of the glass. "You've got to be kidding me," she muttered.

Gibbs's furry tail swished against her calf as he caught up to her, then pulled on his leash toward the front door, all too aware that her mom kept a bag of his favorite peanut butter treats behind the counter. Usually Abbie had to rush Gibbs by, but this time she let him lead her indoors.

"What a pleasant surprise." Her mom, Judith Bennington, lit up at the sight of Gibbs, and knelt to await his overzealous greeting. He'd been known to pin more than one person against a wall with his hefty size. "Hey there, Gibbs." He licked her hand in appreciation, nose nudging toward the counter she stood in front of.

The familiar scent of leather filled the shop as Abbie shut the door behind her to keep the cool air inside. "Mom, did you see what someone taped to your front window? I can throw it away if you want me to."

Her mom stood, brushing invisible dirt from her capri pants. Without meeting her daughter's eyes, she slipped behind the counter and dug out the bag of peanut butter dog treats. Gibbs plopped his rear end down so hard the wooden floor creaked.

"Mom."

Her mother focused all of her attention on getting Gibbs to give her a high five, leaving Abbie to fold her arms across her chest and wait.

She leaned against one of the saddles in its display stand and pinched her lips together to keep her mouth shut. "Why are you supporting the rodeo?" she finally asked, out of patience. Though the shop offered a variety of riding items, apparel, and grooming supplies, it was most famous for their custom saddles.

"It's good for business." Her mom wouldn't meet her lethal glare. Most people weren't brave enough to attempt it. "They set up a whole day for barrel racing. They have mutton busting for the kids—you enjoyed that when you were little. It's not just bull riding, you know."

Mom knew better than anyone why this sign would be upsetting. She'd been by Abbie's side to help pick up the pieces when Logan Attwood chose the rodeo over the life they had planned together. "They'll find you just fine, Mom, even without the poster. Your store has a lot to offer, like the color ad in the paper reads."

Her mom straightened, and after a deep breath, raised her eyes. "The rodeo is coming this weekend whether you like it or not. It'll be good for Starlight's economy. We've never had a *national* rodeo before."

"Stupid reality TV show," she muttered beneath her breath. Ever since camera crews showed up to film a renovation show set in Starlight, everything began to change. Yes, the economy had improved, life breathed back into a town some thought was dying. But reality TV'd brought other things with it, too. Like a franchise chain hotel. An outlet mall. And now the *national* rodeo.

"I've already had a half dozen calls from out-of-town folks interested in saddles, all saying they'll be in town this weekend." Abbie groaned loud enough to turn Gibbs's head. "You wouldn't want us to go out of business," Mom challenged. "Would you?"

Lifting her hands in surrender, she relented. "Fine, I'll drop it." She clipped Gibbs's leash back on and tugged him to the door. His fluffy head kept turning longingly over his shoulder, toward the treat counter. "But don't expect me to like it."

"You can't run away from it, Abbs."

At the door, she paused. It was inevitable. She might be able to avoid *going* to the rodeo, and with any luck, not running into Logan. But the bull riders were coming to Starlight whether she wanted them to or not. "I know."

Outside, the air was stifling for a Wyoming

morning. Or maybe she was struggling to breathe on her own. It would be impossible to hide. Logan would likely waltz back into town, embracing all the fame and glory he'd racked up. The *hometown star,* after all. Even if Vince assigned her to cover every non-rodeo story this week, it wouldn't keep her hidden from sight until Logan came and went.

Her phone buzzed in her pocket.

Erin: Dinner @ 6pm. Making pot roast. Come hungry.
Abbie: I'll be there :)
Erin: Izzy is excited for horse camp with her aunty.
Abbie: Can't wait!

"Well, Gibbs, at least there's some good news today." Her sister-in-law and best friend, Erin, had a knack for cooking Abbie could never hope to achieve. Erin's pot roast was legendary and could cause a person to drool at the very mention.

On her phone, a photo attachment came through, showcasing her niece Isabella in purple cowgirl boots, hugging her favorite stuffed horse, sporting a cheesy grin. Abbie had agreed weeks ago to take her niece to a one-day horse camp that fell on her fifth birthday, just two days from now. At least for one day this week, with Izzy, she'd get a reprieve from the madness of the rodeo traipsing through town.

The *Starlight Gazette* was three doors down from her parents' store. On auto-pilot, she might've missed the front door, lost in thought as she was. But Gibbs yanked her to a halt at the single concrete step. Although he was only allowed inside when the part-timer Carl wasn't in the office—her co-worker suffered from pet allergies—Gibbs knew where he was.

The oversized door and intricate pattern around the windows of the two-story brick entrance were original to the building, built back in 1880. A detail Abbie loved to share with anyone who didn't already know. Historic buildings were a guilty pleasure of hers.

"Someday, Gibbs. Someday."

A couple decades ago, her grandparents owned and ran the *Starlight Gazette*. As a kid, she loved to read the paper from front to back, pride and awe at the thought that Grandma penned most of those words herself. Abbie decided at a young age that she wanted to be just like her.

Though the newspaper had stayed in the family, currently run by her uncle Vince, she was years away from ever *running* the paper. For now, she was happy writing articles featuring her name on their byline. But someday she'd be the editor-in-chief, just like Grandma had been.

"Someday," she said once more. She slipped under the jingling bells of the heavy door and prepared to embrace the chaos Monday morning was sure to bring.

———

"Excuse me?" Abbie sat up straighter in her seat at the round conference table and waited for Vince to clarify. Surely she heard him wrong. Of all the stories to cover this week, he couldn't really assign her *this* one.

"You're assigned to the bull riders, Abbie. But most importantly, I want you to get an exclusive interview with Logan." Vince peeled off his glasses and tossed them on top of a stack of newspapers. "I know you two have a history."

Just a past, committed relationship. But details.

"I need you to set aside any grudges you two may have and do your job."

"We haven't exactly stayed in touch." She spoke the words through gritted teeth, afraid where this conversation might lead. Especially in front of the small staff. Though Carl might not have shown much interest, Jamie, their summer intern, perked too high in her chair for Abbie's liking. "Aren't there any other riders I can interview? How about Cole

Matthews? He's ranked number two right now. I bet I could get an exclusive with him."

Vince leaned back in his chair, running a hand over his forehead. Never a good sign. Always meant he was losing his patience with Abbie. "He's not the hometown star of this rodeo. The people of Starlight want to read about Logan Attwood. To remember the boy he was, read about the journey he's been on. How he's following in his father's footsteps, and how he's finally worked his way to the number-one ranking. In the *world*. Abbie, this is the biggest news story in town this week. Maybe of the whole summer."

"I can do it," Jamie piped up in the moment of silence that followed.

"No," she and Vince said together.

Carl squirmed in his chair and adjusted his glasses, always shying away from confrontation.

A tornado of emotions churned inside her. An exclusive on Logan Attwood could be an opportunity to advance her career. To show her uncle she was ready to take on more responsibility.

Through the glass wall into Vince's office, his nameplate caught her eye. Someday, that would say *Abbie Bennington*. She sighed. "It has to be me," she said, softening the sharp tone she'd aimed at Jamie a moment ago.

"He's turned down all requests for interviews. No radio stations, online articles, video clips, newspapers," Vince added.

Well, that posed a slight obstacle.

"What makes you think he'll talk to us?" Carl asked.

Vince looked at her with expectancy.

"Me." She shook her head. "You think he'll talk to me."

Logan still sent the occasional text, despite her resolve not to answer. She was the one to slam the door in *his* face after he begged her to stick it out. Though they hadn't spoken since that awful night two years ago, she suspected he might be willing to talk to her now if she reached out.

She sighed, wondering how much trouble she'd get in if she simply wrote the article without actually interviewing her subject. She knew enough about his entire life up until two years ago to bluff her way through. What she didn't know she could find online.

"The rodeo hasn't been in town for almost a decade. This is a big deal for the *Starlight Gazette*. We need to be on the pulse of this story. A national rodeo could really put our town on the map. This story could help increase our circulation numbers. Give businesses more reason to buy ad space."

Vince didn't have to spell out the importance of ads in their small twelve-page paper. Though he'd yet to teach her a thing about the business management side of things, she knew without the ads, they might not be able to make payroll for their small staff.

Why did Logan have to be ranked number one right *now*? He'd spent years competing to earn that spot, but always fell a few places short. "An exclusive, huh?" Would Vince be as adamant if Logan was ranked thirteenth instead?

"I'm sure I don't need to mention that other media outlets will be crawling all over Starlight. This Logan interview gives our paper an edge over our competition." Vince thumbed through his notepad. "Jamie, you'll cover the barrel racing. There's a meet-and-greet scheduled for Thursday afternoon."

"Got it."

"Carl, I want you on the mutton busting and greased-pig contests."

Carl, ever the quiet one, simply nodded and jotted down his task on a notepad he carried everywhere with him.

Vince turned to Abbie. "We're covering the front page of next week's paper with an exclusive of Starlight's own rodeo star." He ripped a sheet from his notepad and stuck it out for her. The expectations and parameters of her assignment, no doubt. "I'll talk to the rodeo sponsors. Any questions?" He paused only briefly, to put his glasses back on. "Abbs, your life this week is the rodeo, as lived by Logan Attwood. Where he goes, you go."

The entire week? Her stomach dropped into her toes. It was bad enough she'd probably be expected to cover Logan's performance at the two-night event.

"All of it?" She barely heard her own voice it was so quiet.

"Riders'll be arriving within the next couple of days. Some may've already slipped into town." Vince pushed out of his chair, his large frame towering over the small conference table. "The second Logan gets into town, you find him."

The phone rang, causing Jamie to spring from her chair. "I'll grab that at my desk." She darted into the next room. Carl slipped out right behind her, no doubt sensing the tension.

Abbie hoped it would be a few days before Logan showed up. He didn't have many friends here anymore, and he and his grandfather weren't on the best of terms. That thought was a bright note in all this. Why would he come to Starlight any sooner than he had to?

"Abbie, you do a good job on this, we'll start talking additional responsibilities. Really learning the business, but you got to prove you have what it takes. I know you want to run the *Gazette* someday. Prove you can put grudges aside for the sake of our readers. This is your ticket, kiddo."

"The rodeo, huh?"

"With an emphasis on Attwood." Vince scooped up an overflowing manila folder and tucked it under his arm. "Unless you do want Jamie covering it instead?"

"No!" she replied with a little too much zest and

11

desperation. Jamie was a bright kid, and she'd proven helpful in her short time with them. But there was no way she'd be outshined by an intern.

"So, what'll it be, then?"

She craved the responsibility of managing the *Starlight Gazette*. But most of all, she wanted the freedom to write and print the stories that were near and dear to her heart, like her grandma used to. Vince had turned down more than one of her heartfelt articles as of late. Several, in fact.

"I'll do it. I'll get the interview with Logan."

CHAPTER 2

*L*ogan

It'd been two years since Logan Attwood last stepped foot in his hometown of Starlight, Wyoming. Two years since he'd been healed enough to ride a bull again after one nearly killed him. Two years since the woman he'd planned to spend the rest of his life with slammed the door in his face.

He slowed through town, looking around for changes. Much was the same. The scarcity of stoplights, the house on the outskirts of town with llamas in the yard, the house across the street from that with a meticulously kept lawn in crisscrossed mowing patterns.

The Starlight Grill looked packed to the brim if the overcrowded parking lot was any indication. His stomach rumbled at the thought of a big, juicy steak. He'd have to grab one before the week was over. But stopping in now would announce to everyone he'd snuck into town a few days ahead of the rodeo crowd.

It'd been years since Starlight hosted any kind of rodeo, and never a national event. At a stop sign he waited, engine idling, debating whether to swing by the old grounds. Curious to see how they'd managed to revive the place that'd sat abandoned for so long. His buddy Cliff and his family were expecting him, though. Twenty minutes ago.

Almost on cue, his phone buzzed.

Cliff: You close?

Before he rolled forward through the vacant intersection, he sent a reply.

He didn't know when he'd see Abbie, but he was willing to bet it wouldn't take long. She'd always been close with her brother, and she adored her niece. He inhaled a deep breath and slowly let it out.

Unless Cliff had warned his little sister that he was planning to stay with them for a week and gave her the chance to go into hiding until the rodeo left town, she'd be around.

His buddy lived on the outskirts of Starlight, the two-story house with a wraparound porch centered on a private, well-treed lot. He had enough time to wonder if Abbie'd even come watch him ride before Cliff's house emerged through a clearing in the trees. He wondered how long the privacy would last. How long would it take for the circuit's paparazzi to find him here?

A little girl stood at the top of the front porch steps, a stuffed horse dangling precariously from the crook of her arm. She studied him with curiosity and caution.

His heart squeezed. *Isabella.* She'd had a birthday a few days after he turned his back on his hometown almost exactly two years ago. That Cliff forgave him for skipping out on that intimate family party was nothing short of a miracle.

Slinging a duffle bag over his shoulder, he exhaled and slammed the truck door shut. He locked it out of habit, though he couldn't imagine anyone in Starlight stealing his riding gear.

"Hey there," he called to the girl. "You must be Isabella."

She stood unmoving, the horse now swinging in her grip. Her bright blue eyes watched him suspiciously.

"I'm Logan. I'm—"

"Daddy's friend." Her demeanor softened a bit, but the grip on her horse tightened. She kicked at the porch, showcasing an adorable pair of purple cowgirl boots. If only he'd given up the rodeo when Abbie wanted him to, maybe they'd have a little one of their own.

He stepped up onto the porch, but before he could dwell on it too much, the front door burst open and Cliff spilled onto the porch. "Hey, man!" Two strong arms wrapped around Logan and squeezed. Cliff clapped him on the back so hard he nearly coughed.

"Good to see you!" Cliff's smile stretched across his face. No hint of animosity at his two-year absence, though Cliff had come out to Vegas last year to watch him compete for the title. "You catch up with Izzy?" He backed up and capped his hands on the little girl's shoulders, ushering her forward.

"She's growing like a weed." Because Isabella was still warming up to him, squeezing that stuffed horse with her death grip and sinking back against her dad's legs, he shoved his hands in his pockets.

"Come on in. Erin's just finishing up in the kitchen. She made a pot roast."

He followed, though reluctantly. Erin wasn't from town. Cliff had found her in college and somehow convinced the city girl to move to Starlight and marry him. She'd grown awfully close to Abbie during the time he was around. Now, he wasn't so sure she'd greet him with a smile. If anyone had tipped off Abbie, it was sure to be Erin.

"Let me take that." Cliff yanked the duffle bag from him. "You're staying in the room down the hall. First door on the left."

The screen door slammed shut, and the knock of boots against the wall drew his attention. Isabella was apparently not allowed to wear them in the house. They sat piled in a corner near the door as she rushed by in a blur, horse still in tow, toward the kitchen.

He waited for a beat, not sure whether he wanted to follow. But he'd best face Erin now and get it over with.

"He's here, he's here!" Isabella announced.

No sense in standing idle now. He leaned a hand on the doorjamb, kicked off his boots, and bravely headed toward the kitchen. "Hey, Erin."

Erin turned, wiped her hands on her apron, strands of her black hair escaping a bun. "Logan." They stared at each other across the kitchen, her expression blank and unreadable. He considered taking his bag and leaving. The new hotel in town might still have something available, especially for one of the top bull riders.

"You have a beautiful daughter," he said finally. He shoved his hands back in his pockets. "Can't believe how much she's grown since I last saw her."

"Izzy, did you say hi to our guest?" A hint of a

smile broke across her lips. He wasn't sure what to make of it.

"Hi, I'm Isabella Bennington," she said from the safety of her mother's apron. One hand was wrapped around Erin's leg. "But you can call me Izzy. This is Tux." She lifted her horse.

"Hi, Izzy. I'm—"

"Logan Attwood. You ride bulls."

"Yes, I do." He flashed a smile to Izzy, winning a giggle. She skittered out of the kitchen. "Is this okay?" he asked Erin, suddenly feeling as if he had to know. "Me staying here?"

Erin folded her arms, taking a slow breath before replying. "I wasn't thrilled at first," she admitted. "But you're Cliff's best friend. If you stay at that hotel, you'll get bombarded." She dropped her hands at the sound of the oven timer and turned toward the stove. "Maybe you deserve it, considering that's part of the price you pay for glory. But it wouldn't sit right with Cliff, so it wouldn't sit right with me, either."

The roast's aroma hit him smack in the face. He hadn't stopped for anything to eat since this morning. Now he felt he could inhale the entire thing. "I do appreciate you putting me up."

"You should know that Abbie lives in the guest cottage now." She pulled the roast pan out and set it on the counter. A push on the oven door closed it. With a hand on her hip, she faced him. "You are to leave her alone, you hear?"

"Yes ma'am."

His eyes traveled through the window above the sink to a small cottage out back. He remembered it well. He understood now why Cliff hadn't offered it up to him this time, as he had all those years Logan spent traveling throughout the season. Before the breakup.

"Abbie's my best friend." She took a step closer and pointed a potholder at his nose. "I picked up the pieces once. I won't do it again."

"I'm starving!" Cliff bellowed, staggering into the kitchen and catching his wife up in his arms. He spun her around to face him and planted a quick kiss on her lips. "It smells wonderful."

Erin left Logan with one last warning glare as she broke free of Cliff's hold. She handed him a stack of plates and nodded toward the table in the window alcove. His eyes kept traveling out toward the cottage he'd called home for so long. Was Abbie there now? Did she know he was here, in town early? Surely Erin would've warned her.

At the fifth plate, he had only enough time to pause before he heard her voice. "Hey, Peanut!"

If he lived to be a hundred, he'd never forget that voice.

Every muscle stiffened as he debated whether to run or turn and face the woman who'd broken his heart. Maybe if he stayed absolutely still, she wouldn't see him.

"Who invited the bull rider to dinner?"

He turned slowly, letting his eyes take in the woman he'd always known he was meant to marry. Except right now her scowl and narrowed eyes didn't promise much. Her hair was longer, a few inches below her shoulders, but everything else about her was the same. He faced the woman he'd loved with his whole heart. Those deep brown eyes, the way she pinned back that strawberry blonde hair just on one side.

"I hope this won't be a problem," Cliff finally interjected. "Logan's gonna stay with us this week to help keep him out of the limelight."

The tension in the kitchen practically crackled. He half expected a bolt of lightning to zap the center of the room. He tried to get words out, the same ones he said to Erin earlier about his willingness to stay at the hotel. But his tongue was tied, and his heart felt twisted in knots.

"He's a bull rider!" Izzy announced, her horse bouncing with her. "Isn't that cool?" She flashed a wide grin to Abbie, and for that, he could have hugged her. He made a mental note to spoil Izzy rotten. Whatever she wanted, it was hers.

Abbie folded her arms across her chest. "A whole week, huh?"

"Just need to take care of a few things before the rodeo this weekend."

Finally, Abbie nodded.

"Why don't we all sit down," Erin suggested. "Isabella, did you wash your hands?"

The girl bowed her head, avoiding eye contact.

"C'mon Peanut. I'll help you." Abbie took the girl's hand and led her away, most likely to a bathroom on the other side of the house from the sound of the echoing footsteps on the hardwood floors.

He looked at Erin. "She didn't know?"

Erin busied herself wiping her dry hands on a towel. "It was better this way."

Better than giving her warning? He wasn't sure he agreed. But he was relieved Abbie hadn't been given an opportunity to leave town before he could talk to her. And now that he knew she was staying this close . . .

He slipped into a chair with a view of the cottage, carefully tucking himself in the corner so Abbie wouldn't be forced to sit too close to him. He couldn't expect her to easily welcome his unannounced presence. Nothing ever came easily when it involved Abbie Bennington.

"My hands are clean!" Izzy announced as she paraded back into the kitchen and skipped to her chair.

"Do you mind if I take mine to go?" Abbie asked Erin. "Vince wants that article finished up first thing tomorrow morning." Her voice was calm now, as though that short break gave her a moment to compose herself. She didn't so much as glance his way, but his eyes never left her.

"Sure, sweetie. Let me fix you a plate."

To-go container in hand, Abbie slipped out without fanfare. His eyes stared at the door for several seconds after it closed, yearning for her to turn around and join them for dinner.

Erin carried the platter with pot roast to the table. His grumbling stomach nearly made him forget about Abbie, until he caught her speed-walking toward the cottage. The door slammed behind her, not surprising to him. She'd always had a bit of a temper, but she was good at concealing it from most people.

"I hope you're hungry," Cliff said, snapping his attention back to the table.

His eyes caught Izzy from across the table. "Starving." Abbie'd been so good with her niece. As much as he tried to concentrate on his delectable plate of food, he couldn't stop picturing her, arms crossed, brown eyes narrowed, hair longer and covering bare shoulders in the sleeveless white blouse.

They'd broken each other's hearts, and he'd hoped to find closure for them both while in town. But being with her in the same room after so much time apart, he was no longer sure closure would be enough.

CHAPTER 3

bbie

"Ugh!" Abbie stomped into her tiny kitchen and tossed the Tupperware onto the counter.

There was nothing she hated more than the rodeo. Except for a certain bull rider staying with her family.

"This isn't happening. This *so* isn't happening." She paced from the open kitchen to the living room and back like a caged lion, fighting the urge to grab her dog and run. Maybe to California or Alaska. She'd be willing to bet they didn't host any rodeos in Alaska.

Gibbs looked back and forth between her erratic

23

pacing and the meal she left on the counter without any hint of when they might eat it.

She no longer had an appetite. Not with the man who'd stomped on her heart sleeping less than twenty yards away. The guest cottage no longer offered enough privacy to satisfy her.

She plopped onto the couch and flipped on the TV. Maybe she could distract herself with an episode of *NCIS*. Gibbs sat at her feet, eyes expectant. Feeling guilty about the cooling dinner she wasn't sharing, she nodded. "Fine, just this once." Gibbs climbed, as delicately as his seventy-five-pound body allowed, onto the couch he frequented when she wasn't home. His fluffy head dropped into her lap.

"Where does he get off staying with *my* family?" she asked with a shout, startling Gibbs. She stroked her dog's head in apology. "It's bad enough the rodeo found its way back to town after all these years. But *this?*"

A gentle knock on her door caused her to stiffen. She couldn't handle seeing Logan. Not yet. Sooner or later, she'd have to face him to request an interview he didn't want to give anyone. But she needed an episode or two to prepare herself to ask the dreadful favor.

"Go away, Logan!"

"It's just me." Erin poked her head around the door. "Can I come in?"

She almost said no. She was just as furious with her best friend for keeping Logan's stay a secret from her until the very last second. Until tonight, she hadn't even realized Cliff and Logan had stayed friends. "Sure."

Lifting the remote, she flipped the TV back off. She hadn't been paying attention anyway. Despite her fury, she'd never been able to stay mad at Erin for long.

"Look," Erin started, raising a plate with what looked suspiciously like her famous cinnamon apple crumble cake. *Probably a peace offering.* "I'm sorry we didn't tell you about Logan staying with us."

Abbie folded her arms, bumping Gibbs's head in the process. She tried to look mad for Erin's sake, but she felt too guilty and started petting her dog instead. "Why didn't you? You didn't think I would like some warning?"

After setting the plate on the kitchen counter, Erin fell onto the couch, in the small gap Gibbs left open. "What would you have done, Abbs?"

Fled town. But she didn't say those words out loud. It would be admitting Erin was right. "You know I don't handle surprises well, even when they're good ones. And this? This was *not* a good one." It was only dumb luck that Izzy needed to wash her hands, and even if she hadn't, Abbie would've dragged her to the bathroom. She needed that minute to gain some composure.

"Seeing Logan so unexpectedly like this . . . it's unsettling." He had more stubble on his cheeks where he'd hardly been able to grow any. He filled out his shirt a little more in the muscle department. There'd been a scar she didn't remember on his neck, peeking out from his shirt collar.

But everything else . . . the swagger, the cool and calm demeanor, those dark eyes . . . everything else was the same. And dang it, she wasn't braced for a surprise like that.

"It's been two years." Erin ran her fingers along Gibbs's back, earning a grateful moan of appreciation. "Don't you think you should talk to him?"

Abbie's eyes widened in disbelief. "Whose side are you on?"

"For closure, Abbs."

"I don't need closure." Although living in her brother's guest cottage, single without any prospects, well, anyone could beg to differ at least a little. But so what? She loved her life. Her dream job as a journalist with a promotion in reach. Tomorrow morning, she had a showing at a house she'd admired for years. She didn't need to wait for a man to start her own life. She'd only ever made that mistake once.

"Think about it, okay?"

Dread washed over her, and she covered her face with her hands. Gibbs licked her fingers in concern. "Vince wants me to interview him."

"Logan?"

She nodded, her eyes squinting shut as though she might awaken from some nightmare if she squeezed them hard enough. "He wants me to write an exclusive for the front page. The *whole* front page."

"An exclusive? Abbs, that's wonderful!"

Opening one eye to make sure it was really Erin sitting across from her and not some stranger in her place, she sat baffled. "Wonderful? That wasn't the choice word I had in mind. Not even in my top ten."

"This is your big break! Don't you see? You've been waiting for a front-page story since you started working at the *Gazette*, and now you have one."

Gibbs wagged his tail, sensing excitement.

"But it means I have to interview Logan. That I have to *talk* to him. Spend *time* with him. Erin, I'm not ready to do any of those things. At the very least, he could've had the decency to wait a couple days before showing up. I haven't even had time to adjust to the idea." Although she was sure a lifetime would still not be enough time to prepare herself for Logan Attwood waltzing back into town.

"Does he know?"

"That's the worst part." Not only did he not know, he would have to be convinced. She knew she could accomplish that, but at what cost? She shook her head. "No."

"When you planning to ask him?" Both Gibbs and Erin looked at her expectantly.

"Article's due Sunday at midnight." The *Starlight Gazette* wasn't a big enough operation to wait until the night before to print. Everything had to be prepped in advance for their weekly edition. It was miraculous enough they circulated one newspaper a week when surrounding communities were struggling to put out one a month. "Maybe I'll talk to him after the rodeo is over."

"Abbie," Erin scolded.

"I could start writing it sooner," she suggested in offering. "I know enough about him." Already the plan sounded solid to her. Easy-peasy. Write as much as she could now. Wait until the last possible second to talk to Logan and fill in the blanks.

"When has procrastination ever worked out for you?" Erin asked. If Abbie tried to argue, her friend would list no fewer than three examples of when procrastination completely sabotaged her. There were plenty to pick from.

"I don't like this," she whined. Gibbs licked her hand again, as if to offer his condolences on the crappy matter.

"Why don't you go talk to him tonight?" Erin said. "Get it over with."

"Tonight?"

"He'll be tied up with his family things tomorrow, or so I overheard. And you have horse camp with Izzy the day after. If you're not careful, that deadline will be staring you in the face with only minutes left. A sloppy article might cost you. Don't you want Vince to realize you're ready for more?"

Erin's practicality won out again, as it had many times during their friendship. It was an odd match but nice balance to Abbie's impulsive nature. "I don't know."

"I could send him out to you."

She narrowed her eyes to dagger points. "Don't you dare."

"Then go talk to him." Erin pushed up from the couch, leaving Gibbs with one last good rubdown. "The sooner you get this over with, the easier it'll be to deal with him around. He's only here for the week, you know."

Logan Attwood never stayed in town for long. That had always been the problem.

————

Abbie allowed herself to watch a full episode of *NCIS* before going to talk to Logan. The storyline was one of her favorites, which was just as well; she hadn't paid attention to more than a few minutes of it. A hint of smoke from the fire pit had drifted through a cracked window halfway through the episode, luring her to peer through the pane of glass. Logan sat only yards away with his feet kicked up, quite at home. "Gibbs, this is a terrible idea."

Her faithful, fluffy Newfoundland mix at her

side, Abbie trekked through the back yard toward the patio. She'd watched Logan push around the fire with a long stick for the last twenty minutes, but she didn't want him to think she was desperate to see him.

She wasn't.

"Hope you didn't let your dinner get cold." Done messing with the fire, Logan was stretched out in a lawn chair, feet propped up on an edge of log. "That was some amazing pot roast."

She stopped just short of the patio pavers, debating whether to let Gibbs off the leash. Her dog wasn't used to being restrained in this yard, but she wasn't ready to find out whether Gibbs was a traitor. "Why are you staying here?" Okay, maybe not the best way to start a conversation that involved a big favor. But it was too late to take back the burning question.

"I wanted somewhere quiet." Logan leaned back a little more in that reclined lawn chair and folded his hands over his stomach, calm and cool as ever. It was what made him a good bull rider. He never cracked under pressure. She hated that she knew that about him.

"You couldn't stay with your grandpa?" It was a loaded question, and she already knew the answer. Their relationship was strained since Logan chose to return to bull riding.

Logan crossed his feet at the ankles, still unperturbed. "Didn't have an invitation there like I did here."

She wondered if he'd been out there yet, if he knew just how sad that place was looking these days. "You shouldn't need one," she said. But he did. Gerald hadn't forgiven him for getting back on a bull a year after one nearly killed him. To the bull-riding community and his fans, Logan was courageous for riding again. But to his family, he was reckless.

"What do you really want out here, Abbie? I know it's not the pleasure of my company."

"You're unbelievable," she muttered. She'd meant to keep it under her breath, but the smirk on Logan's face let her know he heard her. She needed to watch her temper and her tongue if she had a chance at getting an interview for the cheapest price. Maybe it would only cost her a lunch, to catch up. She could handle that. "I have a favor to ask."

Logan laughed his deep, low rumble that always made her heart speed up, even when she was mad at him. "Really, now?"

"I-I'd like to . . . to interview you." Man, she sounded like a stuttering fool. They'd been together for years before the accident. They grew up together. Why was it suddenly so difficult to ask a straight-out question? "For the newspaper."

"No."

"But—"

"I've told everyone, including your boss, that I'm

not doing interviews. I'm not here to be in some spotlight, contrary to what you may think."

She posted her hands on her hips. "You're ranked number one. In the *world*, Logan. The spotlight never leaves you."

He dropped his boots to the ground and rocked forward in his chair to sit up straight. "Ah, so you *have* been following me." She wanted to wipe that smug smile off his lips. When Logan Attwood knew he had the upper hand, he was unpredictable.

"It's all anyone in town has talked about for days." There, that didn't give away the truth—that she'd followed every rodeo he'd ridden in since he left her, if only to make sure he wasn't injured. Or worse, killed. "What's it going to cost me?"

Logan prodded the fire again. "Cost you?"

She folded her arms across her chest, Gibbs's leash dropping to the ground. Before she could snag it up, the traitorous dog sprinted for Logan. Dang if he didn't lean into Gibbs's affections, rubbing the dog with both hands and talking to him as if they were old pals, all the while keeping her dog safely away from the fire.

He spoke into Gibbs's chocolatey fur without looking up at her. "When did you get a dog?"

"You and I both know you're going to do the interview," she said with more confidence than she felt. Doubt had begun nagging at her. He might flat-out refuse. "Let's cut to the chase. What do you want in return?"

Logan stood, pouring a bucket of water on the fire. She'd forgotten how he towered over her. How safe she used to feel with him because of it. "Save your begging." As the fire hissed and smoked, he sauntered toward the back door but paused before he opened it. Gibbs looked back and forth between her and Logan, as if wondering whom he should follow.

"You'll have to tell your boss to find a new front-page story. I'm not doing any interview."

 ogan

When Logan was growing up, the graveled drive onto his grandpa's acreage was meticulously kept up. Fresh mulch, trimmed bushes, perfectly intact split-rail fencing, and always the right sprinkling of wildflowers.

Years ago, there'd been more family living here—Logan included—for a short time after his dad passed. But one by one, those family members passed away, too. First his grandma. Then his mom, never quite recovered from losing her husband from a heart attack. Now, only his grandpa remained there on the outskirts of town.

He felt a clutch in his chest as he rolled along that same graveled drive, now overgrown. Bushes grew rampant and wild. What flowers were left were choked out by weeds, and the washed-out mulch was nearly nonexistent. Pieces of the fence stood broken or missing entirely. "So sad."

Gus, the family shepherd dog that used to run circles around his truck when he came back to visit, eyed him lazily from his shady spot on the front porch as his truck rolled to a stop.

He parked near the garage, mindful to leave the spot in front of the door open for his grandpa.

"Hey, Gus," he called once out of the truck. He waited a moment, hoping the dog would run to greet him the way he used to, but he didn't even lift his head. Logan wondered if it was an omen for how this visit might turn out. Grandpa hadn't seen him yet; he still had time to get back in the truck and turn around.

His heart ached at the disrepair he faced in every direction. Weeds everywhere, a barn in desperate need of a fresh coat of paint, and the roof of the main house was missing more than a few shingles. He made a note to have someone repair the roof before it got worse.

Though his grandpa hadn't spoken to him much in the last two years, every month Logan still sent a check from his winnings to help with the upkeep. But as far as his bank statement indicated, his grandpa had never cashed a single one. Too much pride, he suspected. A family trait for certain.

Gus's tail thudded against the worn porch boards like thunder. It took less than a minute for the front door to fly open.

"What'r'ya doing here?" Grandpa stood in the open doorway, one foot on the porch, the other tucked inside.

"I'm in town." He kept a slow stride, cautious of each step that might result in a slammed door. "Thought I'd stop, see how things are going."

He had a hard time keeping his eyes off all the things that needed attention. In his absence, so much had been neglected. He briefly wondered if it would have been different had he stayed. But he pushed out the thought as quickly as it came. The past was in the past. Nothing he could do to change any of that now.

"Things are fine."

Gus lifted his head at Logan's approach. The heavy gray in his once golden coat jarred him. They'd gotten Gus when Logan was fifteen, but the dog never seemed to slow down. He'd still been racing around chasing rabbits the last time Logan saw him. "You take Gus to the vet?"

"Don't need to. It's old age. He got old while you were out running around the country."

His grandpa had, too. The creases around his eyes had multiplied, the wrinkles deepened. He still had his full head of white hair and prominent, if not notorious, mustache. But the strains of a hard life were evident.

"I could take him if you want, get him a checkup."

"No."

Logan slowly took the few stairs up to the porch, unable to drown out the loud creaking they made beneath the weight of his boots. He wasn't sure whether his grandpa would even invite him in, but he was going to try anyway. "Got any coffee?"

They stared at each other for a long beat before Grandpa relented. "I'll put on a pot." Logan slipped through the door before it could close on him. It wouldn't be the first time he'd been locked out of this house.

The kitchen table was littered with papers, mail, and legal pads, with only a single spot cleared for eating. "How's work been?" he asked as he fought the urge to riffle through the stack of mail. It wasn't like his grandpa to be so unorganized. They'd been raised to put everything away. Everything had its place.

Grandpa dug around in a drawer until he found a coffee filter. "It's work."

"You could retire, you know."

The drawer slammed shut. "If I wanted your opinion, I would've asked for it."

"Grandpa—"

"Still riding them bulls like a fool?"

Bull riding was in his blood. It was all he knew, what called to him when he lay awake at night. It wasn't something an Attwood could easily be talked out of. His grandpa Gerald, his mom's father, had never once ridden a bull. Never wanted to. "That's why I'm in town."

Grandpa laughed, a sneer left on his face. "Knew it wasn't to see me."

Before Logan's nearly fatal injury, his grandpa had been more supportive of his bull-riding career and his desire to follow in his dad's footsteps. He had proven he had the knack, the talent, the fortitude. Everyone had been more supportive when he was earning heaps of money and the injuries were minor.

"I'm here, aren't I?" An envelope with bright red lettering on the outside caught his attention, and he lost his ability to leave well enough alone. "What's this?" he asked, shaking off a couple other pieces of mail in the process. "Final notice?"

Grandpa wouldn't meet his eyes.

"Grandpa. This is a foreclosure notice."

"I know what it is."

"I don't understand."

Grandpa yanked the coffee pot from its stand, the dark liquid sloshing to the rim. "They cut my hours, that's all. I picked up another job, so don't worry about it."

"I've sent you money. Every month for two years."

"I don't want your money."

This was absurd. His grandpa was really willing to let his home go into foreclosure—too proud to take his money? "This is your home." *My home,* he nearly let escape. "It'll get auctioned off. Probably to some developer who'll ruin all this."

"Don't pretend you have all the answers." Grandpa shoved a mug at him. Black was as good as it would get; he doubted there was even fresh milk in the fridge. Grandpa leaned back against the counter, unwilling to join him at the table. "You haven't been around."

His heart twisted. He had no argument to that, so he sipped his coffee instead. He'd always imagined visiting his grandpa here someday, with Abbie. They'd bring their family over for Sunday dinners so the kids could play out in the yard. He wouldn't ride bulls forever. Most riders retired in their late twenties, early thirties.

He'd clung to his dad's advice his entire career, that he never let a bull get the best of him. His nearly fatal ride had cost him a lot. It forced him to step down before he was ready. Worst of all, he'd let a bull defeat him.

Tornado, a nasty black and white spotted bucking bull, would be retired after this season but Logan had yet to draw the beast since returning to the circuit. Time was running out.

"Let me buy it from you, then."

Grandpa sputtered a laugh at that comment, then sipped on his coffee. "What do you want with this place? You're never here."

"You stay on until I retire. You can stay as long as you like." It would take a lot of time and money to spruce everything back up to its former state. Logan had plenty of both.

"No, thanks."

"You'd rather let the bank take it than sell it to me?"

Grandpa poured himself another cup. "I'm tired, Logan. There's too much to do around here, and I don't have the time."

It took a lot of self-control for him to bite his tongue. With the monthly amount he sent his grandpa, he could've hired someone to do the upkeep and general maintenance. "Then let me get someone while I'm in town."

"No."

It was time for him to go before there was an all-out blowout. He hadn't come here to pick a fight. He hoped to help spruce the place up a bit before he left for the next rodeo event. If nothing else, at least line up a crew who could. But his grandpa made it abundantly clear he wasn't needed or wanted.

He dug a VIP ticket out of his shirt pocket and set it on the table. It'd probably get lost in the sea of mail and notepads. "For you. Both nights." He left before his grandpa could tell him he wasn't coming.

Gus followed him with his eyes until he was out of sight. He didn't care what his grandpa said about the dog. He'd come back later and take him to the vet. It was one thing he could control. Everything else in his life was a mess.

 *bbie*

Abbie's realtor, Christy, hesitated at the front door of the Victorian house, hand hovering above the dead-bolt. "I shouldn't have brought you here."

Abbie shoved her hands in the pockets of her shorts to keep from grabbing the key. "You know I *had* to see this house."

"It's not in your budget."

She understood that Christy—dressed in a cute skirt and a sleeveless ruffled blouse, and prepared for a full day of showing homes to clients following this unconventional favor—was only trying to manage her expectations. She wasn't one of the top real estate agents in Starlight for nothing. But she'd broken a cardinal rule she made all other clients abide by: she'd taken Abbie to a house she couldn't afford.

"I know. I just want to see inside."

"Abbie, it's fifty thousand over what you're prequalified for."

"I'll be quick." Vince wouldn't be too happy to hear she was out and about on personal business instead of glued to Logan's side. If her uncle hadn't caught wind that his front-page subject was already in town, he would soon enough.

"It's just a peek. Not a real showing."

Unable to keep still, Abbie let one hand run along a white column of the Victorian home's covered wraparound porch. It could use a fresh coat of paint, but it wasn't anything she couldn't handle. Already, she could envision Gibbs lounging on the porch while she ran a paintbrush along the woodwork.

Her heart had been set on this house for years. As a little girl, she rode her bike by, admiring the sturdy house that stood proudly with its whimsical style. She dreamt of climbing the stairs to the top of the round turret to watch the sunset. But now that it was finally for sale, the price tag was too steep. "No wiggle room on price, huh?"

"It's already at a competitive price."

In other words, someone would scoop up this

house before too long, despite the fact it needed some TLC. "Do I need a bigger down payment?"

"Much bigger. But that's not why we're here, remember?"

It'd taken her three years to save up her nest egg of a down payment, but she wasn't going to let a little bad news make her gloomy. Logan's unexpected presence so close to her current living quarters gave her enough gloom to last the week. "Think I could move in today?"

"Abbie," Christy warned.

"I'm kidding."

Christy unlocked the front door at last, allowing her to step over the threshold first. She slipped off her sandals and rushed into the house, in awe of the grand staircase that wrapped around one side and climbed with the high ceiling. She ran her fingers along the polished banister.

More than once, she had nearly been caught looking in the windows when she was a kid. She'd always wanted to see inside this mysterious, big old house. But all attempts had been unsuccessful beyond a few peeks. She'd even tried selling cookies once, but the old lady who lived here chased her away with a broom.

"You know Mrs. Hampton. She's not really the type who'd budge on price."

"I wouldn't expect that of her." Even now, when Abbie saw the woman downtown, she wore the same stern expression she had years ago. Friendliness wasn't a quality she possessed.

Her fingertips feathered across the decorative molding and textured walls. Though the outside needed some sprucing up, the inside was meticulous.

"The seller isn't willing to do any updating, beyond what's already been done." Christy shook her head. "Why am I telling you any of this?"

Abbie was in love, already envisioning how she'd place her furniture. What pictures she'd hang on the walls. "It's like a time capsule. Look at this gorgeous chandelier! And these high ceilings."

"If you're serious about buying a house, there *are* other properties in town, you know," Christy said. But the words were pointless.

Abbie shook her head. "No, it's got to be this one." She slipped through a doorway and found herself, through a series of twists and turns, in the kitchen. With the stainless-steel appliances and gas stove, it seemed it was the only room on the main floor that had any amount of updating.

"I'm not writing your offer."

"It's a shame they had to take out the original kitchen, but I get it." Abbie traveled slowly around the island in the center of the spacious room, admiring the pot rack that hung over it. She may not be as talented a cook as Erin, but in a kitchen like this, she could try. "I can work with this."

"The seller won't take a dime under her asking price."

"Can't hurt to ask." But seeds of doubt had found their way in. No matter how much she wanted to deny it, Mrs. Hampton wasn't likely to lower her price just to help Abbie's dreams come true.

Christy's phone chimed. "I need to take this." Two steps from the doorway, she stopped. "Wrap it up. We're leaving in two minutes."

Abbie moved to the back door, staring out into the spacious yard and the gazebo she'd admired for as long as she could remember. There was a time she dreamed about sitting out there with her laptop. Dog by her side. Logan tinkering with some crooked board or pesky nail. Or maybe he'd spend his time in the barn or sprucing up the horse corral. He'd always wanted horses of his own.

A blissful life, or it was supposed to be. One that didn't involve bucking bulls capable of killing a man in mere seconds.

"Time to go," Christy called. "I have to go write an offer before the next showing."

Abbie mourned the loss of an opportunity to check out the upstairs and her long-admired round tower. "We can come back, right?"

"Only if you come up with another fifty thousand dollars for your down payment."

"But—"

Christy pulled on Abbie's arm, dragging her back

to the front door. Once they were on the porch and the door was locked behind them, Christy turned to her client. "I didn't want you to get your hopes up, Abbs. There're three more showings scheduled just today. I'm sorry."

"It's okay, I get it." But inside, her heart twisted. She'd waited years for this house to come up for sale. She'd always known it was meant to be—*Ours*. The simple word jolted her. Because she'd always pictured living here with Logan.

———

The overcast sky fit Abbie's dim mood as she walked down the main strip. She really did love this little town and its picturesque downtown. But right now, she couldn't fully appreciate it. Not with the knowledge that her beloved dream house would probably have multiple offers by the end of the week.

Her mom was watching Gibbs, but she wouldn't mind if Abbie stopped off somewhere before she picked him up. Her first instinct was to check in at the office. She'd scanned her emails this morning at home, but it wasn't the same. She thought about it until the moment her fingers wrapped around the metal handle of the *Gazette's* front door.

"What am I doing?" she muttered. She couldn't go in there. Vince would want an update about the interview. No way he hadn't heard Logan was in town. Her uncle had an uncanny ability to learn things before everyone else, a secret she hoped he'd pass along. She wasn't ready to tell him that Logan flat-out refused. She wished it was that easy to get out of the assignment entirely, but she knew her uncle too well.

Letting go of the handle, she walked away, unnoticed by huddled co-workers she saw through the window. She'd stop for a coffee instead.

"Fancy meeting you here," Erin said, bumping Abbie with her shoulder inside the quaint, quirky coffee shop that opened its door earlier that spring. Turning the Page doubled as a bookstore and had become quite the popular spot in town. It was something Starlight had never been able to support before the TV reality show came to town. *Guess it's not all bad.*

She managed a weak smile.

"I'm so sorry, Abbs." Erin wrapped her in a hug as they waited for their orders.

"How did you know?"

"You didn't call me. I had a feeling."

"It's not fair."

"I know you love that house, but maybe it's not meant to be." Erin carried both their cups to a small table near a window next to an endcap of mystery novels. She nodded to Abbie to sit. "A house, especially one that size, is a big responsibility. It's four bedrooms. Almost three acres. The upkeep alone would wear you out. You'll be so busy chasing stories and learning the business . . . When would have time to do all that?"

Abbie let her head drop onto the table, an ugly, frustrated sigh escaping. She'd once dreamed about her and Logan living there together. The upkeep might be a little more manageable if she wasn't forced to do it alone. "There won't be any of that. Logan won't do the interview."

"The Abigail Bennington I know would never give up that easily. You've hardly tried."

Running her hands down the sides of her face, Abbie groaned. "I'm not going to make a fool of myself. He'd get too much enjoyment out of that."

"Maybe."

"*He* left. He's the one who walked out on what we had. I'm not going to suck up to him just to get an interview." But she was lying to herself. That interview could be the stepping stone she needed to someday run the *Starlight Gazette*. Without it, she might never realize that dream. Big stories like this didn't come often to Starlight. There was no telling when the next one might be. The thought made her stomach turn. She pushed away her untouched coffee.

"Logan left," Erin repeated, "but you're the fighter. The bulldog. You've always been able to get what you want. You're persistent. That's what I love about you most, Abbs."

. . .

Erin's words stuck with her as she closed in on the saddlery store to pick up Gibbs. She was able to get almost anything she put her mind to. Almost anything, except the man who left her behind.

"I hope Gibbs has been a good—"

"He's been an angel." Logan flashed his megawatt smile the camera and his fans loved, forcing her to divert her attention to a display of equestrian books. She picked one up off the rack and flipped through the pages.

"What are you doing here?"

"In the market for a new saddle."

She rolled her eyes. "For *what* horse?"

"Maybe you mean *which* horse. I have a few."

It occurred to her that she knew a lot less about Logan's current life than she realized. She didn't even know where he called home these days, despite vigorous efforts to track down that piece of information. She could start that article, but she'd never be able to finish it without his cooperation. *Dang it!* "Where exactly?"

Logan chuckled, that deep rumble. She busied herself with adjusting a button-down shirt on a hanger. That laugh always made her come undone. Every time. It wasn't fair that years later he still had an effect on her at all.

"I'm not giving that up so easily." He pushed off

the counter he'd been leaning on. "You might want to stalk me."

She huffed a laugh, but her jittery fingers knocked three shirts to the floor. "Stalk you. Please." She crouched down to pick up the clothing, giving herself a moment to catch her breath. *Ridiculous. This is so ridiculous.*

"Can't trust just anyone these days."

"I'm just doing my job," she said as she stood back up, finding Logan much closer now than a few moments ago.

"Still stuck on that interview, huh?"

She shrugged, looking around the shop for her absent dog. A scattering of brown dog hair blanketed the floor around Logan and trailed to behind the counter. She discovered Gibbs asleep back there, his massive body resting against the cupboard door to his favorite treats.

"What's in it for you anyway?" Logan asked. "You wouldn't agree if there wasn't something you wanted out of it. I'm not stupid, Abbs."

Debate bounced in her head. Should she admit a promotion of sorts was on the line? Would he even care that it was that important to her? "They didn't think you'd talk to anyone else," she finally said. It may not have been the whole truth, but at least it was only a lie by omission.

"And Vince thinks I'll talk to you." Logan laughed, waking Gibbs this time. The dog lifted his head, turning it from side to side until he caught sight of her. His furry tail thumped against the floor as he let out a sleepy yawn and struggled to his feet.

"I know, crazy." Gibbs stretched, then trotted to Abbie for a greeting hug.

"How did you end up with Gibbs?" Logan asked. "Didn't take you for the big-dog type. Especially not one that'll be the size of a miniature pony by the end of the year."

She almost told him about meeting the dog no one was willing to adopt at the local shelter while writing a story. He was too big and everyone worried how they'd handle him when he doubled in size. She only had to meet him once to know they were destined to be together. But Logan didn't need to hear any of that. "Did you stop by your grandpa's?"

His smile faded, his lips dropping into a frown. "Yeah."

A silence hung in the shop as she waited for more. Did he know about the foreclosure notice? She had caught a glimpse the last time she dropped off a newspaper to Gerald. She wanted to mention Gus, how he needed to see a vet. But if she knew Logan, he already came to that conclusion. He'd always had a way with animals.

"Abbie, hey!" Her mom rushed in from the back room. "Sorry, Logan, had to take a call about a special order. I can't tell you how good this rodeo has already been for business."

"I'm glad to hear it, Mrs. Bennington."

Mom smacked him playfully on the arm. "Logan, you know you've always been able to call me Judith."

"Yes, ma'am."

Abbie rolled her eyes. "Oh, brother."

"We all set on that saddle order?" her mom asked Logan.

"Yes, we are." He flashed that smile again. The one that made all the fawning young girls squeal as if he were a pop star only too kind to grace them with a minute of attention. "Just had one more thing."

"Yes?"

He fished something out of his shirt pocket. "Tickets."

"You don't have to do that!"

"VIP seating. Special behind the chutes tour on Saturday. Dinner with the cowboys."

"You have got to be kidding me," Abbie muttered. "Mom, you're not seriously going, are you?"

"VIP seats, Abbie."

The smirk Logan wore made her blood bubble. Her mom had always loved him. She'd been there for her when he left, but the man would always hold a soft spot in the heart of Judith Bennington if her sparkling eyes and giant smile were any indication.

"There's a ticket for you, too, Abbs."

"Give it to someone else." She clipped the leash on Gibbs, prepared to fly out the door. She didn't know where she was supposed to go since the office would never work. Possibly home to start writing an article. Maybe she could get Erin to squeeze the details from Logan over family dinners if Abbie planted a digital recorder in the kitchen.

At the door, Logan said, "If you promise to come to the rodeo, we might be able to talk about an interview."

She inhaled a deep breath. She'd expected a price, of course, but she wasn't sure this was one she could afford to pay. She couldn't handle watching him on a bull. She'd followed his career via online stats, but she'd never watched a video of him giving more than a brief interview. She tried once, and it gave her a panic attack. She kept imagining him getting crushed by the bull that nearly took his life.

"And if I say I don't know?"

"Then let's start with lunch."

Lunch she could handle, even though she had no idea what rabbit hole it might lead her down. "Okay. Lunch."

CHAPTER 6

*L**ogan***

Most everyone Logan knew believed him to be calm and collected in every aspect of his life. On a bull, he was. But around Abbie Bennington, his heart never ceased to race at a hundred miles per hour.

"You look good, Abbs." She looked like a dream, sitting across the table in Mabel's Diner with sunlight illuminating her wavy locks. They'd come here often in their first months of dating. It was an old favorite, and judging by her nervous hands rubbing her arms nonstop, she hadn't forgotten.

"You'll do the interview if I agree to come to the rodeo?"

That was his Abbie, always right to the point. But he couldn't let her off the hook that easily. He reached for his glass of iced water, leaned back in his seat, and sipped. "When did you move into the guest cottage?" She'd lived in an apartment a block from the main strip when they parted ways.

Irritation at the delay flashed in her eyes, and he couldn't hide the smile at her inconvenience. She sure was cute when she was mad.

She scanned the diner. "Have you seen our waitress?"

He learned a long time ago that she didn't let anyone in easily. He'd been lucky to break through her walls all those years ago, but she'd fortified them again, this time much stronger. He calculated what it'd take to bust through once more, and whether Erin's wrath was worth the risk. "Abbie."

"I'm dying for a strawberry lemonade," she said, still scanning, still avoiding him. She tucked a wavy lock of hair behind her ear.

Though he didn't need a menu, never had, he pretended to look through his anyway. The lunch options were the same today as they'd been years ago, but it bought him time to rethink his strategy. He hadn't expected her to be so standoffish when that article obviously meant a great deal. "How long have you had Gibbs?"

Unable to successfully flag down their server,

Abbie let out a sigh and answered. "Got him almost a year ago. Shelter dog."

"Really?" Maybe it was because she had lived in an apartment that wouldn't even allow her to own a goldfish when they were together, but the massive dog was a surprise. "How'd you decide that?" he asked as their server approached them.

"Hi, Sasha," Abbie said in greeting. The relief was visible from across the table, her shoulders dropping, her frown relaxing into a smile. He hadn't realized being left alone with him would be such torture for her. "Can I get one of those tasty strawberry lemonades? I've been craving one all day."

"Sure thing." The waitress looked expectantly at him, and he ordered something—anything—to get her to leave.

"Since when do you drink soda?"

Ah, that finally got her attention. He rarely drank soda of any kind, but today he didn't care. "So, you do pay attention."

"Journalist." She busied herself digging in her oversized purse. He wondered if she was looking for something that didn't exist. But eventually she pulled out a spiral notebook and a ballpoint pen. She scanned a page filled with notes. "I already know the basics." She flipped a couple more pages, those filled too.

"What's all that?"

"Everything I know about you." She rocked the

pen in her fingers as she skimmed through what she'd already jotted down. "For the article."

He tried to be his cool self, tried to let it go. But it made him uneasy how much she'd already compiled without his help. If he wasn't careful, she would collect the couple of personal details she was lacking and be out of his life forever. A week ago, he'd have accepted that fate, but not now.

"What else do you want to know?" he asked cautiously, afraid she might see right through his question for what it really was.

"Home base, what you do when you're not doing the rodeo, what you hope to accomplish, who you might be dating." She looked up from her notebook, ice in her narrowed eyes. "When you might *retire.*" Sasha interrupted the uncomfortable tension hanging between them with her drink delivery.

Once they ordered their entrees, he decided to try another approach to get her to open up. "How're your mom and dad doing?" Maybe it was only a stalling tactic. The woman he'd always love sat across him in the booth, and he wasn't ready for this to be the last time. He just didn't know what to do about it yet.

"You were just talking to my mom this morning, weren't you?"

"Didn't get a chance to ask too much." He sipped at his soda, already regretting the choice. It usually made him so thirsty. He pushed it away and went for the sweating glass of iced water instead. "Surprised your dad wasn't around the shop today."

Relieved was the truth. Judith had a soft spot for him, but Mr. Bennington was another matter entirely. He made it clear that if Logan returned to bull riding after he recovered from his injuries, he might as well write himself off. Abbie's dad was a hard man, but he was a fair man. He loved his daughter very much.

"He's at some saddle convention in Tulsa this week." Abbie flipped back and forth between a couple of notebook pages. "You're lucky."

"He wouldn't approve of your front-page assignment?" He let a smirk fall across his lips, because they both knew it was true. And it seemed to irritate her, which he enjoyed to no end. Yes, he was the one to go right back to the rodeo life after he healed. But she was the one who told him to stay gone.

Abbie fiddled with her napkin, slowly unrolling the silverware. "He'll understand. It's business."

"So is the rodeo."

She squeezed her fork until her grip turned her knuckles white. "Not the same."

"It's my *career*, Abbs. Something worth noting for that article you hope to write," he said with a nod toward her notebook. "Tell me how it's not the same."

"Because you didn't have to choose a career that

puts your life in danger every single time you compete."

They'd gone round and round days before he left two years ago. He'd tried to make her understand why he had to go. Tried to make her understand that until he rode Tornado again and lasted eight seconds, he'd never be able to quit. But she hadn't wanted to hear any of it. It was something he feared they'd never see eye-to-eye on, especially not with all the time that'd gone by. "It's who I am. It's in my blood. Just like the newspaper is in yours."

She started to rebut that, but Sasha delivered their entrees. It gave him the moment of pause he needed to redirect their conversation. They'd get nowhere by arguing. And if their heated conversation got any louder, their corner booth might not be so private.

He wasn't ready for the entirety of Starlight to know he was back in town. It was important for him to win here in his hometown, and the national title if he could. It would be an accomplishment in honor of his dad, but he didn't enjoy the spotlight that came with it. It was something he entertained for the sake of his sponsors.

Abbie poked at her chicken pecan salad. "So, you went to see your grandpa?"

"Yeah." It didn't seem possible for a house that'd been in the family for decades to be involved in foreclosure proceedings. Why his grandpa took out a line of credit rather than use the money Logan had been sending him, he'd never understand. Pride had never gotten anyone anywhere. "Wasn't too happy to see me."

"You're surprised?"

"Not really." He wanted to tell her about the foreclosure notice. Ask her advice on how to convince his grandpa to accept the help he needed. But it'd been a long time since Logan was able to do that. How many nights had he picked up the phone, only to realize Abbie'd never answer him?

"What's it going to take, Logan?" she asked after a long pause.

"For what?" But he knew. He was trying to buy himself time. Every minute with Abbie was more precious than he could describe. The longer he spent in her presence, the more he wanted her back in his life. It'd caught him off guard, but she'd always had that allure about her.

"For you to do the article."

Finished with his lunch, he wadded up his napkin and dropped it on the plate. "If you want me to talk, Abbs, you're going to have to spend some time with me. I'm not just going to fire away a bunch of rehearsed answers."

"But—"

"You can start by making it to family dinners. Tonight. No more skipping out."

She huffed. "If I show up, you'll start talking to me about the article?"

"Come to dinner." He left some cash on the table and slid out of the booth. "Don't be late."

———

Logan sat with Cliff in his truck as it rolled along the graveled road toward the Holbrook Ranch. His buddy had to make a delivery for the saddlery to a loyal client and invited him along for the ride.

His nerves still rattled from that lunch. He'd been a fool to think Abbie'd eventually relax around him, but he yearned for it just the same. Couldn't stop thinking how he might accomplish just that.

"You can wait in the truck if you want," Cliff said. "Lina will probably demand an autograph if she spots you."

Before he replied, he caught the mischievous smirk Cliff couldn't hide and stopped himself. "How're the ranches doing around here?" he asked, referring to some of the bigger local spreads. In some areas he'd traveled, they were being bought out by large corporations. He hoped Starlight was spared that travesty.

"Surprisingly good." Cliff slowed for a turn. "Most of them still in the right hands."

He was glad to hear it, even if Cliff might be leaving something out. The ranch he had grown up on, only a few miles from the Holbrook place, was sold shortly after his dad died. With the amount of debt it'd amassed, his mom couldn't afford to keep it. He was too young back then to get a job, so they moved in with his grandparents.

He hoped the new owners had made themselves a true home there. A place where their kids could run wild for generations to come. His dad had hoped for the same thing for them, but it hadn't been in the cards for their family.

"I'll just be a minute." Cliff shifted into park and hopped out.

Logan fiddled with his phone a minute, the temptation to text Abbie nearly overwhelming. It had to be that he was back in Starlight. There'd been moments since he returned when it felt as though everything was still the same. As if time had somehow frozen itself during his two-year absence and nothing changed.

But everything *had* changed. That was the problem.

Discovering he didn't know what to text, he jumped out of the truck instead to lend Cliff a hand. His buddy had tried to save him the attention but it'd come sooner or later, whether he wanted it or not. Lina, he hoped, would be glad to see him.

"Thanks for your help back there," Cliff told him as

they left the Holbrook Ranch an hour later. Lina, as expected, had talked his ear off. But it felt good to know someone in town was excited to have him back. Luckily, he had a couple extra tickets to leave with her—she smiled quite broadly at that.

At the end of the drive, he couldn't fight the pull. "Think you could turn down that road?" He wanted to see what the ranch had become. Even if the new owners had let things get a little overgrown or rundown like his grandpa's place, he wanted assurance that a family was happy where he'd grown up.

"Logan, I'm not sure you want to—"

"Please?"

Cliff sucked in a sigh, gave a curt nod, and turned onto the graveled road Logan used to ride his bike down. He wondered what Cliff wasn't telling him.

Tall trees intermittently lined the road, and Logan smiled. He'd taken Abbie down this road in an old beat-up truck he'd had back then, more than once. Even taught her how to drive a stick shift, and tried not to panic when she nearly ran them into an ancient oak.

They'd parked in the ditch that evening and watched the stars in the glow of the moonlight from the tailgate of his truck. He couldn't take her to the ranch, but it was almost the same thing. "The same stars I watched from the roof outside my bedroom as a boy."

They spent years together, but in the blink of an eye, it all disappeared. He hadn't realized how badly he still wanted it back until he saw her last night in Cliff's kitchen. They could have the life they'd always planned, if only she could let him finish his rodeo career first, the way he needed to.

"Some things've changed," Cliff finally said as they drove up on the property. But Logan had to look twice, because it didn't look like the right place.

"You sure this is it?" It wasn't remotely recognizable. It didn't look like someone's home at all. Not with the convoy of cement trucks, concrete silos, parking lot filled with cars, and layer of white dust that seemed to coat everything within a hundred-yard radius.

Cliff rolled to a stop on the grassy shoulder. "Happened about a year ago."

"What happened to the family that used to live here?" But only a strong-willed memory could conjure vague images of what that might've looked like. The factory erased all evidence of such a thing.

"Last I heard, they packed up and moved out of state. Ranching life . . . it wears on people. Especially those who don't really know what they're getting into. I think they gave it a solid effort, but they just weren't cut out for it."

Just when he thought he'd seen enough, Logan caught sight of a familiar dusty red pickup and his heart dropped. Since when had his grandpa started working at a cement factory? He'd been one of the most sought-after mechanics in Starlight for decades. Was this really the second job he mentioned?

He had to look away before he completely lost it. "Let's go."

bbie

"Ugh! Gibbs, maybe you should take a stab at this. Can't make it any worse." Abbie'd wasted an entire afternoon typing up everything she knew about Logan, but no matter what angle she used to approach the story, it sounded like garbage. Her article was a disaster. She was pretty certain Izzy could write a more compelling article.

Gibbs looked up from his comfy dog bed, all four limbs spilled out. He let out a soft doggy moan. She knew he'd outgrow the extra-large dog bed, but she hadn't expected it to happen so soon. At this rate, she'd need to buy him a twin mattress.

"You're sure a lot of help."

She went back to typing what was her third draft of the day, trying to ignore the ticking clock. The hands warned she didn't have much time before Erin had dinner ready. She had no choice but to show up, or she'd probably not only get passed up for advancement, but fired as well.

She'd hoped to find a way to spend as little time with Logan as possible. But her grand idea to flesh out ninety percent of an article and sprinkle in new details about his recent life had blown up in her face. It was unreal how little was known online about the man. There were certainly more gaps about his previous life than she realized.

"You'd think someone would've figured out where he lives," she muttered.

Though Logan didn't deny he was dating anyone when she dropped that comment at lunch, and she hadn't been able to find a girlfriend captured by the paparazzi, it unsettled her anyway. It was possible some flashy girlfriend might show up at the end of the week to cheer him on at the rodeo. The thought caused her to ball her fists at her sides.

Gibbs perked up his head, and a few seconds later, someone knocked. Gibbs beat her to the door, blocking her way and attacking her with his swishing tail. "You have to let me answer it, buddy." She nudged the dog-slash-bear cub with a strong shove of her hip, and opened the door a crack.

"Ready for dinner?"

Logan Attwood stood on her doorstep, his intoxicating, woodsy cologne drifting in through the narrow opening. He'd always looked like a million bucks in that cowboy hat, dang it. She wasn't ready for the jolt her body felt.

"I have five more minutes." It was a weak defense, but she needed each of those minutes to catch her breath. It had escaped out the door, probably now lingering somewhere around those smoldering eyes. "I'll meet you inside."

"I can wait."

"Um, okay." She pulled Gibbs back by the collar, removing his pushy nose from the gap and closing the door. If Logan wanted to wait, he could wait outside. Gibbs rushed to the window, hoping to spot his new friend. She leaned against the door and let out a giant breath.

She startled at another knock.

"Abbie?"

"What?"

"Can I come in? It's hot out here."

She twisted a lock of hair in her twitchy fingers. "Cliff has A/C."

"You can ask me one question."

Bribery. She stared at her laptop mocking her on her coffee table. How many words had she written and deleted today? One good question could fuel a half-decent rewrite tonight. "Any question?"

"Sure. Just let me in, please. I need some water."

She opened the door before she could talk herself out of it. Gibbs charged, tail knocking the TV remote from the arm of the couch in his mad dash to greet Logan. She didn't try to stop him. If Logan wanted in, Gibbs was part of the deal.

"Hey there, buddy," he said to the dog once the door closed behind him. He reached into his pocket and pulled out what looked suspiciously like a bone-shaped treat. "Can you sit?" Gibbs plopped his bottom down, eager eyes waiting for him to toss the treat.

"Steal that from my mom?"

Logan lifted his head, meeting her gaze. "Is that the one question you want to go with?"

"No," she fired back immediately. "Glasses are in the cupboard to the right of the sink. Help yourself." She skittered back to the couch and pretended to finish something up on her laptop. But she kept stealing glances at Logan in her kitchen. There'd been a time in their lives when such a sight was common.

As he gulped his water, she scrambled to decide which question would help her the most. Everyone in town wondered where he lived. She'd overheard more than one coffee shop conversation last week, speculating whether he bought a fancy ranch some-where out west or if he found himself a mansion in some flashy city. He'd won enough money to purchase both.

"Well?" Logan asked from his side of the kitchen island.

She carefully crafted the question in her mind, worried she'd ask in a way that could be answered in only a couple of words. "Can you tell me about your home base?" It was entirely possible he had multiple properties with the amount of money he'd won over the years. He saved most of it when they were together, and these last two years, he'd won quite a bit more according to the online stats. "Where it's at, what it's like, that sort of thing."

Logan shook his head, that irritating smirk showcased across his lips. "That sounds more like two questions, Abbs."

"You're kidding me."

"Pick one."

"What?"

"Do you want to know where or what?"

"What would it take to get the answer to both?" she asked, already dreading the answer.

"I have something in mind."

She closed her laptop and popped to her feet. Gibbs, the traitor, hadn't left Logan's side since he stepped into her cottage. "Start with where. *Where* do you live?"

"Place near Albany."

"New York?"

He gave her a funny look at that. "You really think I'd move to New York?"

"Albany, Wyoming," Abbie said.

"Yes. Can we go now?"

Why did it surprise her that he still called Wyoming home? She hadn't been to his town in years, but as she recalled, it was hardly a four-hour drive south from Starlight. So close to home, she could there and back in one day. She quickly banished that particular realization.

"Even Gibbs is ready," Logan added, coming closer to usher her out the front door.

She zipped toward the door before he could successfully place his hand at the small of her back. She was still recovering from his unexpected presence and that darn cologne. He'd worn it on their very first date, back when they were just teenagers. Because she told him she liked it, he kept wearing it.

"Do you own a ranch near Albany?" she dared to ask as she closed the door behind them. Gibbs darted for the back door of the main house.

Logan just sent her that smirk. "Dinner. Let's go."

———

Erin slid a steaming pan of lasagna onto potholders on the table. The aroma of baked cheese made Abbie's stomach rumble, and she realized she hadn't eaten anything since her salad with Logan. She'd been holed up in her cottage, focused on the only thing she could control: the article going nowhere.

"Smells fantastic," Logan said, winning a smile from Erin. "I haven't eaten this good in a long time. You're gonna have me spoiled by the time I leave."

The reminder that he *would* be leaving soon shouldn't pack such a punch. It should feel like relief. The sooner he finished his competition this weekend, the sooner he could go and leave her alone. Let her get back to her normal life.

"Tomorrow's my birthday," Izzy announced, bouncing in her seat next to Logan. She normally sat beside Abbie, but somehow the bull rider had won her over, too. Abbie assessed him from across the table to figure out his secret. He had to be bribing Izzy with something.

"How old are you gonna be?" Logan asked, his attention completely given to the little girl. Abbie hated to admit how sweet it all was.

Izzy unclenched her fingers and held out a flat palm. "Five!"

"That's practically an old lady!" Izzy giggled at that, so Logan teased her even more about grown-up things, earning a wrinkled nose of disinterest in growing up. Abbie wished she could reclaim that kind of naïve innocence. A lot less heartache existed at that age.

"Aunty Abbie is taking me to horse camp!" Izzy declared, hopping up in her chair. She hugged her stuffed horse and rocked from side to side. Her curled ponytail swung with her.

"Sit," Erin demanded as she set down a plate of breadsticks and took a seat at the table. Izzy obeyed.

"Where's Cliff?" Abbie asked.

"Working late tonight," Erin answered, but with the way she refused to glance up, and instead focused on everything else on the table, Abbie wondered what was up. There was something Erin wasn't telling her. It was rare that her brother worked late for their parents, but possible since their dad was out of town. She almost asked, and might have if Izzy wasn't sitting at the table.

"Are you coming, Logan?" Izzy asked.

Logan held out a plate to Erin and waited for her to scoop up a piece of lasagna. "What's that, now?"

"To horse camp!"

Abbie's throat clenched shut. No. No way. She shook her head at him, trying to keep the gesture subtle but seen. "Peanut, I thought it was just going to be me and you tomorrow." Knowing she'd have most of the day a few miles from town—with no cell service, and with no Logan Attwood—had kept her sane today.

"Pleeease!" Izzy begged, dragging out the plea.

"I think just you and your Aunty Abbie should go," Logan said. "You don't want some ol' bull rider there."

Abbie felt a beat of relief that he was on her side.

She chanced a glance at Erin, but her friend seemed distracted and no help whatsoever in this little debate Izzy stirred up.

"Yes, I do!" Izzy continued. "Please, please, please?"

Erin's phone buzzed on the counter, and she shot up out of her chair. "I'll be a minute." Abbie followed her friend with her eyes, but remained in her chair. Erin obviously wanted her privacy, but she couldn't help her concern. She'd talk to her later, in private.

"But it's my birthday tomorrow!" Izzy pleaded, her bottom lip sticking out in a pout. The threat of tears shone in her bright blue eyes.

"Okay, I'll come," Logan said.

"Yay!" Izzy's frown turned into an instant victorious smile.

"Because it's your birthday." Those words were directed at Abbie, almost in apology. But the twinkle in his eyes didn't suggest a sincere apology at all. In fact, he seemed pretty happy about the whole thing.

She glanced back and forth between the two, wondering if this little episode was premeditated.

Logan gently kicked at her foot beneath the table. "Abbie, she's four."

"Five tomorrow," she retorted. Eerie how after all this time it felt as if he could still read her mind. "You know word'll get out that you're back." It was a weak attempt to talk him into changing his mind, but she had to try.

"No one will bother me out there." Something more unsaid danced in his eyes. "Besides, Lina Holbrook already saw me earlier today. The whole town probably knows by now."

She swallowed. If one of the most prominent figures in Starlight knew he was back, Vince did too. Maybe Logan coming along to horse camp might save her some grief, even if it threatened her sanity.

"Sorry about that," Erin said as she came back into the kitchen and sat down. The smile pasted on her face was for show, but Abbie wasn't fooled. She'd not call attention to it now, though. Erin might not want to air her dirty laundry in front of Logan. "Cliff should be home in an hour, but he said not to wait."

"Everything okay?" Logan asked.

Abbie kicked him under the table, a little harder than she meant to, judging by the size of his widening eyes.

"Yep, fine." Erin scooped lasagna onto her own plate. "Please, don't wait to eat on my account. Dig in."

"We have to leave at seven," Abbie said to Logan to draw away attention. She tried to say that without a groan, but she wasn't sure she was successful. Horse camp was an all-day event for five-year-olds. Instead of escaping him, she'd be stuck with Logan for far too many hours.

"Logan's coming to horse camp!" Izzy told her mom, bouncing in her seat again. Her stuffed horse fell on top of Gibbs who lay on the floor beside Izzy's chair, but he didn't seem to notice. The dog knew it was the best place to catch falling food and remained on alert for anything he could eat.

"Is he, now?" Erin raised an eyebrow at that, looking back and forth between her and Logan.

"Izzy insisted," Logan said.

Erin smirked, shaking her head. "That'll be something."

Abbie reached for a breadstick and tore it in half. "Yeah. Something."

CHAPTER 8

With his pledge to answer another question, Logan knew Abbie wouldn't stray far after dinner. She'd taken Gibbs back to the cottage with the promise to meet him at the fire pit in ten minutes. But they wouldn't be staying home tonight. No more backyard small talk. If Abbie wanted some real meat for her article, she had to start playing by his rules.

He paced in the kitchen as he waited for Erin to put Izzy to bed. The little girl was beside herself with excitement for tomorrow's horse camp.

He'd given it all a lot of thought and was determined to win Abbie back. At first, the idea struck

78

him as crazy; coming back to Starlight had only been about the rodeo and finding closure. But with Abbie back in his life, even briefly, he hadn't been able to put to bed the desire that they belonged together. That he would pull out all the stops this week to help her see that.

Once he accomplished what he needed to this season, he would retire. He could promise her that. Right now, it may not be enough, but maybe in a few days, she might change her mind.

If after the week was over, she didn't want to rebuild what they lost and start their life together, he would walk away for good.

"I think she's finally down." Erin let her words out with a huff of exhaustion. "For now."

"I hope it's okay that I'm going tomorrow," he said. Erin seemed okay with it at dinner, but she'd been distracted. "Izzy was pretty insistent."

"Yeah, she gets that from me, I suspect." Erin folded her arms and leaned against the door jamb, sizing him up. Assessing. Making him feel small and vulnerable. "I'm not thrilled about it," she said. "But I think you two need closure. Abbs does for sure."

He bowed his head because there was warning in her unsaid words. It didn't change his resolve any, but Erin didn't need to know that yet. "I don't want to hurt her, Erin. I never wanted that."

"But you did. You—" Her phone buzzed against the granite countertop, and in a step she swiped it up, leaving the rest unsaid. Whatever Cliff was up to tonight, it had his wife on edge. Logan replayed the conversations he had with his friend earlier today, but nothing lent any clues as to what might be happening.

Now out in the back yard, Erin's words hung with him as he waited for Abbie to emerge from the cottage. He'd loved Abbie Bennington more than life itself. He'd never wanted to hurt her. Somehow, he'd help her understand why he left. That was the plan tonight anyway.

The fluffy chocolate dog shot through the door first and made a beeline for the back door of the house. The soft lug reminded him of a giant teddy bear, if bears had floppy ears. Logan shook his head. He'd always loved dogs, and they'd talked about getting one that could play with Gus once they were married and had a house together. But he never pictured Abbie adopting one that would grow to the size of a miniature pony. In a few months, Gibbs would swallow up half the cottage interior.

Wiping sweaty palms against his jeans, he stepped outside to meet them halfway.

"Why can't I find anything online about your place in Albany?" Abbie asked when she was within earshot. She'd changed since dinner, dressed down in a pair of jeans, flowy tank top, and a pair of sandals. He found he liked this casual look a lot more than her professional attire.

Gibbs rushed him then, and Logan had to crouch down to prevent the dog from colliding into his legs and knocking him down. He rubbed Gibbs in greeting. "Because you're the first one who knows about it."

She fiddled with a pen before finally placing it behind her ear. "You're telling me no one in that town has leaked anything? Ever?"

"I'm not exactly a movie star," Logan said. "Folks around there are nice. They respect privacy." Unlike the little town of Starlight, eager for an invasive interview. The newspaper hadn't been the only media outlet hungry for a story.

"Do they even know your real name down there?"

Logan smirked as he got back to his feet. Gibbs seemed satisfied enough with the attention, so he plopped down and leaned against Logan's legs. "That sounds like another question, and considering I just gave you a freebie . . ."

Abbie let out a sigh, relenting a lot easier than with her previous attempts. "What do I have to do?"

"Come with me."

"It's close to sunset." She glanced toward the unlit fire pit. "Where are we going?"

He winked, then headed for the gate. His truck was parked on the other side, near the garage. He hoped she'd follow. Hoped the enticement of another question was enough for her to trust him. "You'll see."

"Logan."

He ignored the warning hanging in her tone, and kept walking. "Gibbs can come too."

"He'll shed all over your truck."

Yes, he would. But that was a price he was willing to pay. Besides, the furry giant was growing on him. He almost asked what Gibbs thought about the water, but he didn't want to tip Abbie off while she still had a chance to escape. This had to work.

"I've got a blanket back there."

He waited until they were a mile from town before he spoke again. "Think Izzy'll sleep a wink tonight?" It wasn't his best, but he didn't want to leave Abbie too much opportunity to ask questions right now. She'd never agree to this if she knew what he was up to.

A sliver of a smile crossed Abbie's lips. A smile he'd missed so much. "Doubtful."

"She's adorable." Logan sucked in a breath. "I hardly recognize her, she's grown so much."

The smile faded and Abbie stared straight ahead. "That's what happens when you leave and don't come back."

In another time, he would've taken her hand, given it a squeeze, and found a way to make her understand. But too much had passed between them since. Patience, he told himself. Patience was his only shot at a second chance with Abbie Bennington.

"I didn't want to stay gone," he said, keeping his voice calm and even. "Just didn't feel welcome."

Slowing for a turn into a recreational area, he rolled down a back window for Gibbs. No doubt Abbie caught sight of the sign that read *Shimmering Lake Recreation Area.*

"Why are we here?"

He placed both hands on the wheel to keep himself from brushing away a stray wavy lock clinging to her chin. "Because you want an interview." He flashed a smirk at her before parking the truck and hopping out.

"I never agreed to *this*."

So she'd spotted the canoe tied off to the fishing dock. It was a little ricketier than he expected, but for a last-minute favor, he couldn't complain. He just hoped it'd hold all three of them without sinking.

He reached for a couple of blankets, using his body to keep Gibbs from shooting out from the back of the truck like a massive bottle rocket.

"Gibbs won't fit in there," she objected.

Since Abbie still had his leash, he closed the door to keep Gibbs secured in the back seat. "Sure, he will," Logan said over his shoulder as he made his way to the ramp to make sure. *Barely.* The dog would have no room to turn around, but he'd fit.

"He's never been near the water," Abbie hollered

down to him. But she clipped the leash on and let him out of the truck anyway. Gibbs's fluffy brown tail bounced in happiness. It was one step in the right direction.

"Good time to introduce him, don't you think?" He situated the blankets in the canoe, unfolding one enough to make a spot for the dog. No telling if Gibbs would stay put or end up capsizing them, but either might work in his favor. The lake wasn't that deep, and there were towels in the truck if the worst should happen.

"Logan, I don't know—"

"Abbs, look how excited he is."

Gibbs was zipping in zig-zags, tail swishing, negating any objections she might still have. "He's your responsibility, then." She extended the leash, leaving it dangling from her outstretched hand. "I'm not liable for anything that happens."

"Hey, buddy." Logan knelt to hide his smile at the prospect of wrapping a drenched Abbie in a beach towel. And of holding her in his arms to keep her warm. Gibbs gave him a big, sloppy lick on the cheek.

The dog was not about to be contained, but he hesitated at the edge of the ramp when Logan encouraged him into the canoe. "Why don't you get in first?" he suggested to Abbie. "It might help reassure him."

She took a couple steps, close enough the honey

scent of her shampoo drifted toward him in the slight breeze. "You promise to answer another question?"

"Yes." He held out his hand to help her in. "Get in."

"Two?" she asked, ignoring the hand offered.

He slyly traced a finger along her chin, tipping her face toward him for a moment. Something flashed in her eyes. *Longing.* He glanced at her lips, tempted. So tempted. "Don't push your luck, sweetheart," he teased. Though he yearned to draw her in for a kiss, into his arms as he'd thought about for months, he backed away and broke the contact between them.

She stepped into the canoe, careful to keep her face turned away, but he'd caught a glimpse of those flushed cheeks. He hid a victorious smile as he waited for the boat to stop rocking. Despite their turbulent ending, he now held out hope. He still had an effect on her that she couldn't deny.

"Your turn," he said to the dog. Gibbs looked at him, then Abbie, and back again. He started to pedal backward toward the shore, nearly knocking Logan off the little ramp.

Abbie crossed her legs at the ankles, resting her hands behind her along the edges of the canoe. She wasn't about to offer help. "I don't think you're going to get him in here."

After a couple more failed attempts and a lot of

whining, Logan fished a treat out of his pocket, catching Gibbs's full attention.

She shook her head. "Did you steal a whole bag from my mom?"

Ignoring her, he sat along the edge of the ramp and set his feet in the bottom of the canoe. He stretched his hand toward the blanket he set up for the dog and dropped the treat. "Go get it, boy!"

Hesitation gone, Gibbs leapt after the morsel quicker than Logan anticipated. The small boat rocked as if hit by a massive wave, eliciting a squeal from Abbie. "Logan!"

He clutched the edge of the canoe, using all his strength to steady it before she or Gibbs fell overboard. The lethal glare she shot his way once everyone was righted made him laugh. She sure was cute, all riled up like this. Man, he missed that.

"It's not funny!" But she was having a hard time holding in her laughter, and through those pursed lips, a smile broke free. "You realize we all could be drenched right now? Including Gibbs."

Treat gone, the dog perked up at the mention of his name, tail wagging. It took a second treat to convince him to lay down.

They laughed together as Logan untied them from the little dock and paddled out toward the middle of the lake. It felt remarkable, this unguarded moment between them, an experience he worried they'd never share again. Even if Abbie refused to forgive him, at least he had this one memory to carry with him. That radiant smile, brighter and more breathtaking than the setting sun.

"You laugh," she finally said now that she'd calmed herself, "but it'd be your truck that smelled like a wet dog."

"Are you sure he's a dog?" He turned the canoe toward a small offshoot creek they knew well. He suspected Abbie might already know what he was up to, but if she did, she didn't try to stop him. "Think he might be part grizzly bear or something?"

"No one wanted him, you know." She stroked Gibbs along the back of his neck. So far, he was doing okay sitting in the canoe and watching, though his inquisitive eyes kept locking on the reeds in the water. Hopefully, he wouldn't leap out after any. "At the shelter. They weren't sure what to do with him."

"Where did he come from?" he asked, wondering how a Newfoundland ended up in a Starlight shelter.

"Someone dropped him off late at night." Her brown eyes dimmed. "They attached his leash to the bench right outside the door, and that was it. Not even a note."

"That's terrible."

She shrugged. "There're worse places they could've left him."

He didn't want to think about that. All in all,

Gibbs was one lucky dog. "What are you going to do when he doubles in size? He'll outgrow that cottage."

He watched her lips part, as if she were about to tell him something important. But she looked away instead. Twisted a lock of hair around one finger. She'd let her guard down for a few minutes, but for some reason, it was back up. "I'll figure something out."

"He's very lucky to have you, Abbs."

"Spoiled rotten is more like it."

"You've always had a big heart." He wished there wasn't a dog between them so he could reach for her hand and give it a squeeze. But putting Gibbs on one end or another was a recipe for disaster, especially if he decided something in the water was more enticing than hanging out in the little boat. Keeping him in the middle kept the weight balanced.

"I did a story about the shelter." Abbie bent her knees and folded them into her chest, wrapping her arms around them. He couldn't tell if she was cold or just relaxed, but she refused the blanket he offered. "I wanted people to know about these wonderful dogs. The shelter was getting full, and they weren't sure what they were going to do."

Gibbs eased into position, resting his head on Abbie's feet.

"That's the kind of stories you always wanted to write." He remembered long conversations about the differences she wanted to make with her written words. The lives she hoped to touch, and the hope she wanted to showcase.

"Vince didn't want to print it."

"What?"

"He didn't think it would help sell papers. The shelter didn't have ads with us, so . . ."

Abbie had worked at the *Starlight Gazette* since her high school days, when she was an errand girl with a paper route. She'd worked her way up through the ranks, but she and her uncle had always had slightly different views on how the newspaper should operate.

"Your grandma would've printed it, no doubt about it."

She relaxed into a smile, some fond memory dancing through her mind, no doubt. "Yeah."

He steered them down the creek as the sun disappeared beneath the horizon. The nearly full moon had lingered low in the sky, just waiting for the stars to make their debut. He wondered if she remembered what very special events had taken place all those years ago, right here.

Their eyes met across the canoe as Gibbs began to snore. They shared a quiet chuckle, and for a moment, he believed things could be repaired between them. Could they still have the life together they'd planned?

"You remember."

Her body stiffened, eyes locked on the sleeping

dog between them for several tensely silent moments. "Is that why you brought me here?" Her quiet words seemed shaky.

"This place—"

"We can't go back, Logan. That's not how this works."

"I've never stopped loving you, Abbs."

She looked away, clearing her throat. "Then why did you lie?"

"Lie?" This wasn't working out as he imagined. "I never lied."

"You said you were done." Her words came out in a growl. "You said you wouldn't go back."

"I—"

"But you . . . *left*." Her voice cracked, and he knew what that meant. Tears were silently falling, and he wanted nothing more than to comfort her. But such an attempt, tonight with the dog between them and her upset, would surely send them all into the lake. All this time, and she believed he lied to her.

"I never said I was done with the rodeo."

"But—"

"*You* said I was. *Everyone* did. I'm the only one who never said I was done."

 bbie

The next morning, Abbie was awake much too early. She'd always been an early riser, but this particular day arrived a little too soon for her liking. She'd spent half the night tossing and turning, replaying too many memories—both past and present—through her mind. Replaying those words.

I'm the only one who never said I was done.

Even Gibbs seemed confused about their extra-early wakeup. Now he dozed, in and out of sleep from her couch.

Logan had taken them to a very special spot, one that had a lot of history. He confessed he still loved her, and unraveled the one thing she'd clung to most in her anger when he left.

"You could've at least capsized the boat, you know," she said to the pile of fur on her couch. But his twitching paws meant Gibbs was down for the count.

That spot . . . She sighed. She'd fought all night to keep out the memories, but they burrowed their way back in anyway. They shared their first kiss there. Logan first told her he loved her there, in the moonlight. They shared their dreams of the future, sitting nestled in a canoe with the moonlight glowing on the lake.

She closed her laptop and hopped up from the couch. She'd kidded herself about working on the article this morning, but not a single word had escaped her fingers. She'd forgotten to ask her promised question last night anyway. Sure, Logan was more forthcoming about his season thus far, but it wasn't helping her put aside the whirling thoughts in her mind. If it weren't Izzy's birthday, she'd call in sick and lock the door.

Intending to fix herself a cup of coffee, she somehow ended up in her bedroom digging through her top dresser drawer. A thud sounded from the other room, announcing Gibbs before she saw him appear, stretching his enormous body in the doorway. He let out a groan-worthy yawn.

The small velvet bag had remained tucked away

in the farthest corner of her drawer for two years; she hadn't once sought it out. But this morning, she had to see it.

The ring fell into the palm of her hand, stunning her into silence much as it had the first time Logan showed it to her. He'd been so nervous, she remembered, that he almost dropped it in the lake. They laughed about how differently the night might've turned out if he'd been forced to fish it out.

Gibbs licked her elbow.

"Things were different then, you know?" She let herself fall on the edge of the bed. Gibbs rested his head in her lap, sniffing at the ring she pinched between two fingers. The single square-cut diamond on a white gold band was simple, the way she preferred it. Logan knew her so well.

A banging at the front door caused Gibbs to perk up, knocking the ring from her hand as he abandoned her in the bedroom. She jumped up from the bed, but the ring clattered to the floor and rolled beneath her dresser. "Crap!" She dropped to her knees and shoved her hand underneath, but found the ring too far out of reach.

Gibbs barked as the pounding continued.

Reluctantly, she left the ring and hurried to the door.

"We're ready!" Logan announced when she swung open the door. He and Izzy stood on her doorstep, smiles beaming from them both. Gibbs licked Izzy's face, earning a giggle. Then he leaned his body against Logan's legs, soaking up the attention, no sign of tension from what was said the night before.

She briefly wondered how heartbroken her dog would be once Logan left again. Because despite everything that happened last night, he would leave.

"Happy birthday, Peanut!" She tried to ignore that alluring cologne, but it swarmed around her.

Izzy swung her stuffed horse back and forth in a death-grip of a hug. Her long blond hair was braided into pigtails and they swung with her beneath a cowgirl hat that was almost too big.

"I still need to drop off Gibbs—"

"He can ride in the truck," Logan said. "He seems to enjoy it. We'll drop him off with your mom on our way."

She scooped Izzy up in a big hug, rocked her back and forth while little legs swayed in the air. She continued until Izzy's giggling filled the air, then set her down. "Are you excited to be all grown up?"

"I'm five!" Izzy shot out her hand, palm flat, displaying five fingers. "I can go to horse camp now!"

"You sure can." She dared a look at Logan. She didn't want him to know that their moonlit canoe ride haunted her all night long. Or that the ring he gave her rested somewhere beneath her dresser because she felt compelled to take it out of its hiding spot. "I'll meet you guys at the truck. Just have to grab a couple things."

Logan winked and said, "We'll be waiting for you," forcing her to look away. She wanted to be annoyed, but truth be told, a tiny part of her was thrilled. It meant that despite everything, he didn't hate her.

Allowing Gibbs to trot after them, she closed the door. She'd gathered all her things earlier this morning, before the sun came up, and even wrapped Izzy's present, something she always forgot to do until the last minute.

After one more failed attempt to fish the ring out from beneath the dresser, this time with a hanger, she relented. Maybe Cliff could help her move the heavy piece tonight. He was the least likely person to badger her about the reason she'd kept the ring in the first place, a question she refused to answer even to herself.

———

Horse camp was a fairly new addition to the Anderson Ranch, started up within the past five years. The idea had saved the ranch from foreclosure, and now dozens of kids from all over the country came throughout the summer. Abbie'd already researched it for the article she planned to write.

They drove beneath a wooden arch decorated with horseshoes and old wagon wheels, a picture she definitely wanted to capture.

After finding a parking spot, Logan briefly touched the top of her hand. "You seem nervous about something."

Her first attempt to answer tangled up in her throat. She wasn't prepared for the electrified sensation of his touch. She swallowed and tried again. "Vince doesn't know I'm writing this article."

"Seems like a common theme." His lips sat in a straight, disapproving line.

"The Andersons aren't interested in placing an ad. They don't need one." So Vince would be extra unimpressed that she asked their freelance photographer, Jillian Harper, to meet her out at the ranch later this afternoon. Izzy grabbed both of their hands and tugged them toward the welcome sign where a gaggle of kids waited. As requested, Mrs. Anderson had tied a few purple balloons in honor of Izzy's birthday.

"Why is everything about ads with your uncle?"

"Without them, the paper wouldn't survive. He considers a story about an annual horse camp filler." Not something readers would rush to buy a paper over. Or so he'd told her a couple of weeks ago when she mentioned doing a write-up on them during her visit. But deep down, she suspected he wasn't thrilled about offering free advertisement to a business that didn't need the boost while it refused to return the favor to the *Gazette*.

She wished her grandma were still here, if not calling the shots, at least able to give her advice. Before Logan pressed further, they were greeted by Mrs. Anderson herself.

"This must be the birthday girl! Welcome, Izzy." Her attention turned from the little girl to the cowboy. "Oh my, we have a celebrity joining us today?" Martha Anderson's hands clapped together as her smile spread wide across her face. "Abbie dear, why didn't you warn me?"

"Last-minute arrangement," she answered. But it didn't really matter what she said, because Martha was fixated on the man in the spotlight. She might've told her that aliens had landed a mile over, and Martha would've just smiled at Logan in a distracted haze.

"He's a bull rider!" Izzy piped up.

"He sure is. Ranked number one, you know. Our own local rodeo star!"

"I'm just Logan." His attempt at humility seemed to win Martha over even more, but it made Abbie roll her eyes.

"Are you ready for horse camp?" Martha asked Izzy.

The bubbly birthday girl hopped up and down, her eyes twinkling. "Do we get to ride horses?"

That elicited a wide smile from Martha, and she

reached out her hand. "We'll get to that later today. First, we have to learn how to take care of them. Why don't you follow Ms. Emily?"

Izzy glanced once at Abbie, as if for permission, then followed a teenaged girl toward the group of kids. "Have you ever brushed a horse before, Izzy?" Emily asked.

"Is there somewhere I need to go to check us in?" Abbie asked a very distracted Martha. The woman couldn't seem to keep her eyes off Logan.

"The kids will be so excited you're here—" Something about the word *us* seemed to jolt Martha mid-sentence. She lowered her sunglasses, eyes bouncing back and forth between Abbie and Logan. "You two are back . . ."

"No," she said immediately. The last thing she needed was an entire camp of kids catching wind of a false rumor. It was bad enough having Logan in town for the week, but she didn't need talk of them to continue once he left. That gossip had been hard enough to endure last time. In a small town, everyone seemed to assume they knew the whole story.

"Always thought you two were meant to be together. The whole town thinks so, you know. It broke our hearts when you split up."

"I'm here for Izzy," Logan said much more smoothly, easing that smile back onto Martha's face and switching the subject. "She's my best friend's daughter."

"Well, we're very glad to have you as a special guest today." Finally, Martha looked at her and pointed. "Registration's inside that cabin."

With the frenzy of an unannounced celebrity gracing the Andersons' horse camp, Abbie wondered if the article she hoped to write would be forgotten. She started to mention it, but then stopped. Between Logan and a family with four kids approaching behind them, Martha was much too distracted. Though Vince would encourage a more aggressive approach to capturing a story, she always found patience went a longer distance. She'd find Martha later.

"If your secret wasn't out before, it definitely is now," she said to Logan as he followed her to the registration cabin. "Whoever Lina Holbrook didn't get to yesterday will know you're back before lunch."

"It was going to happen sooner or later." Though the same suaveness he'd used while speaking to Martha remained, something dimmed in his eyes. She'd always thought he loved the fame despite his claims he didn't, but now she wasn't so sure.

"You've always been a talented bull rider, but why is being number one so important to you?" she asked, her question gentler in tone than any of the others she'd asked of him. "I don't remember that ever being something that mattered to you. Not much anyway."

Half expecting him to dodge her or give some quip about earning the answer, he surprised her. "Other than doing something I think my dad would've been proud of? It's something I have some semblance of control over. I can always improve."

She didn't understand. She wanted to, because maybe if she did, she could make peace with the reason he went back to it. Find that closure Erin insisted she needed. She hadn't been able to make sense of the *why* last night. "But you can't control how a bull will behave. What mood he's in or what he might do . . ." She let her words trail off because they reached the cabin to get checked in. But mostly, because she couldn't put her worst fears to words. Not today.

"Abbs—"

"I'll make sure the article doesn't say anything about you chasing number one for the fame or the money, I promise." It was the only promise she could make right now. She turned from him then, forcing him to catch the door or have it slam in his face, and busied herself with Izzy's registration.

———

After the orientation for the youngest kids, they were ushered into the stable to learn about the different types of brushes for grooming horses. Abbie hung out at the edge of the stable, able to see Izzy sitting still and alert.

"She must really love horses," Logan said. "I haven't seen her sit still for more than ten seconds since I got here."

"She does." A warm smile fell across her face as she stared ahead at the red and white mare at the front of the demonstration area. "She's getting one for her birthday, you know. A horse."

"Really?"

"Don't tell Cliff or Erin I told you that."

"I won't."

"Cliff hasn't picked her up yet, but he's got a mare reserved." Abbie couldn't wait to see the excitement and glow in Izzy's eyes when she discovered she got the horse for her birthday. She'd been asking for one for months. "Horse camp was supposed to be a compromise, as far as Izzy knows. They told her she couldn't have one until she was ten."

"But really she's here to learn how to take care of her future horse." Logan leaned against the door frame, folding his arms and crossing his legs at the ankles. He looked so at home that for a moment she forgot they weren't together.

"I think it'll be really good for her. If she's going to lose interest in the whole idea, it'll happen today before Cliff spends anything." She caught sight of Martha again, lingering in the background of the instruction session. She wondered if now was an opportune time to ask her a few questions. She didn't want to get in the way, especially since there was no guarantee Vince would ever let her print this story.

"I went to horse camp once," Logan said, cutting her attention away from Martha long enough to lose her again. "Summer I turned twelve. My dad thought it was important that I learned to care for a horse, even though all I wanted to do was ride bulls. Taught me a lot."

"You seem a little nostalgic," she said carefully. "You must've had a good time there."

"Had my first kiss, you know."

"What?" She smacked him on the arm, but not hard enough to cause so much as a flinch. "I thought *I* was your first kiss." Heat rushed to her cheeks when she realized what she said. Out loud. It shouldn't matter to her anymore.

"You were the first kiss that mattered."

"I—"

"There you are!" Martha snuck up behind them, startling her enough to make her jump back a couple feet. The woman had to be part ninja. Though Abbie hoped she was here to discuss the interview, Martha's eyes were completely set on Logan. "I was hoping you might be willing to say a few words to the kids."

"Me?" Seemed Logan still had that celebrity

innocence mastered, because Martha practically melted.

"Yes, yes! Come, please."

Logan winked at her over his shoulder as he let Martha lead him away. She pulled him for a walk outside, probably to discuss what those words should be.

———

Abbie waited by the truck for Logan and Izzy after she finished up with Jillian, the photographer for the article. Most of the other younger kids had gone home an hour ago. As much as she didn't want to admit it, she was glad Logan had come along. Otherwise, she might never've convinced Izzy to get off her horse.

As it was, Abbie spent most of the afternoon glued to the fence, watching the older kids prepare for a horse show.

Logan had a real gift, she noted. Why couldn't he do something like that instead of riding bulls? Sure, it wasn't as thrilling. But surely he could feel how rewarding teaching a little girl to ride a horse might be.

A myriad of pings went off in her purse like a bundle of fireworks. The Anderson Ranch was not known for its stellar cell phone signal, and she'd spent most of the day without a single bar. But now, reality was catching up.

Most of the texts and the two voicemails came from Vince. Horse camp hadn't even adjourned before he found out Logan was back in town. At least his excited messages ended by applauding her efforts to get their interview subject to come with her to the event.

It was the second voicemail, however, that gave her pause. The rodeo planned a few dedications on opening night—tomorrow—intended as a surprise for those being honored.

Her eyes fell on Logan and Izzy. The little girl hung like a rag doll over his shoulders. She'd had a full day and would no doubt sleep during their drive back to town. With the way the media portrayed Logan, no one would ever suspect he had this wonderful way with kids. They liked too much to play up his being single. The ultimate heartbreaker. Family man was a role most probably didn't even know he wanted. Izzy had taken to him so quickly, so without question.

"This is one tired birthday girl." Logan nodded toward the truck door, and she opened it. Izzy's eyes fell the rest of the way shut the instant she filled in her booster seat, the grip on her stuffed horse tight as ever. "This was a great thing you did for her."

Logan's soft, genuine smiles had always meant the most to her. Unlike the celebrity smile he flashed for his fans and the camera, this sweet one felt unguarded. "I'm afraid of what taking her to the rodeo will do," she admitted.

He nudged her shoulder. "Think we might have a future barrel racer on our hands?"

"Maybe," she replied, though she wasn't really invested in the topic. Her heart twisted. Should she tell him about the dedication for his dad? Much like her, Logan didn't do well with surprises. Yet Vince might demote her back to errand girl if she let out the secret.

"What's on your mind?"

She forced a smile. "Just tired."

ogan

For the second night in a row, Cliff still wasn't home an hour after dinner.

With a yawn, Logan slipped out the back door. It was definitely too warm to light the fire pit tonight, so he simply sat in a lawn chair and folded his hands in his lap. He tried asking Erin about Cliff once Izzy was tucked into bed, but she dismissed his worries with a shrug.

"He's just helping out with some stuff," she said. "Why don't you go see Abbie about that article?"

From his chair, he couldn't help but see the guest cottage. He'd spent a lot of time living there when he was traveling home between events. Even before his injury, his grandpa hadn't been too crazy about the way he set off to make a living. It caused less friction to stay in the cottage and visit the ranch.

With the lights off in the cottage, he wasn't sure where Abbie'd disappeared to. He hoped to see her again tonight. Wished he'd tempted her with a couple more questions she could use for her article when dinner was over. But she practically flew out the back door, Gibbs running to keep up with her.

He stirred the ashes in the fire pit with a stick, thinking back to something an unknowingly wise little girl asked yesterday at horse camp.

"I don't want to leave." He expected the whine after such a long day for a little girl, and practically had to peel her fingers from the metal rungs of the fence.

"You can come back next year."

"I can?"

"Yes." He hoped he wasn't making promises that couldn't be kept.

"Will you come, too?"

"I don't know what they would need me for."

Izzy stared at the ground as they moseyed away from the kids practicing for their horse show and toward the parking lot. She was getting tired, so he scooped her into his arms. "Do they have a camp for bull riders too?"

That question had been on repeat in his mind ever since. Something about it nagged at him.

His phone buzzed in his hand, bringing him back to the present.

Abbs: Meet me at the arena.

He sat up straighter, certain he imagined the text. For two years, he'd waited for a response of any kind, but Abbie's name never once flashed on his screen. He texted her every night for a month when they first parted ways, begging her to reconsider.

Hands that were normally steady typed out a shaky response.

Logan: When?
Abbs: Now

He contemplated the various reasons she might have to meet him at the arena, of all places, and what struck up this instant demand of his time. He suspected whatever her motives, they included getting more information for that article of hers.

But what if there's more?

He slipped into the house long enough to grab his keys and Stetson. He could hear Erin down the hall, talking quietly to Izzy about horse camp, and decided to leave a note instead of disturbing what was surely a valiant effort to coax an overstimulated little girl back to sleep.

It wasn't until he spotted the sheriff parked across the street from the town mart that he realized he'd been speeding through town. He yanked his foot off the gas and let his truck slow on its own. A glance in his rearview mirror assured him he wasn't being followed. He had no idea what Abbie was up to, and he didn't want to delay himself from finding out.

He'd dreamed about her texting him, telling him to come back home. It wouldn't have mattered where in the country he was, he would've driven nonstop until he made it to her doorstep. If only she'd asked him. He thought he'd finally closed that chapter of his life at the start of this season on the circuit, but he was wrong. His heart would always feel as though Abbie was home.

The arena that had looked so neglected and rundown for years, even when it was in use, seemed surprisingly clean and flashy. The setting sun caught on the aluminum of the new grandstands, twice as high as the old wooden ones. Even the parking lot sported a fresh layer of gravel and a serious lack of overgrown weeds.

Abbie stood at the fence, leaning against it. A satchel hung over one shoulder, resting against her hip. He was certain she heard him pull up, but her attention was on the arena. He could tell from here that the dirt was freshly graded, definitely something that'd been brought in for this event.

"It's amazing," he said to her once he reached the fence. She didn't startle at his presence, so he kept talking. "This place looks brand new. Even the shark cage is new. Unbelievable."

"Some things are the same, though." She brushed back a strand of her hair and tucked it behind her ear. He missed kissing that neck and how she giggled at how his stubble tickled against her skin.

He leaned against the fence, careful to leave a little distance between them. Without it, he might be too tempted to put his arm around her and pull her close. "Why did you want to meet me here?"

"You see where the chutes are?" She nodded forward, but it was hard to see them from this distance. The main gate, though, had a padlocked chain around it. If they wanted in, they'd have to crawl over the fence.

"Yeah."

"They're original."

Thoughts spun through his head as he tried to figure out the real reason she dragged him out here. With how passionate she'd been about him never going back to the rodeo, he didn't expect her to end up at the arena on her own—or at all, for that matter. "Original?"

"Almost everything else is new, but they kept the original chutes. Shined them up a little bit. Dedicated them to past local riders."

He swallowed, already sensing where this was going.

"There's one for your dad."

Suddenly he had to see it, the urge overwhelming and too much to keep at bay with reason or logic. He hopped the first fence before he had time to consider his actions.

"Logan! What are you doing?"

"C'mon." He waited on the other side for her to climb over and join him. She kept sneaking glances over her shoulder, but he waved her over. "No one's coming."

"They have *cameras*, Logan."

"So? We're not taking anything. Not vandalizing anything." He flashed her a smile, and saw her breaking. She'd always been one to follow the rules, and breaking them made her a little paranoid. But he had always been able to push her outside her comfort zone, and she never once regretted letting go of her fears. Not with him.

"Logan, we should go."

"What? We just got here. You can't lead me to *this* arena and expect me to leave two minutes later, Abbs." He sauntered up to the fence and reached a hand over the top in invitation. "C'mon. Show me that the brave Abbie Bennington I once knew still exists."

"She didn't have a job she was afraid to lose should she get arrested!"

"If you want to play it safe, stay here."

"I'm not staying here by myself!"

He shrugged and turned away, and made it three steps before she relented.

"Fine. I'm coming."

He held out his hand without forethought of what that contact might do to him. Her hand gripped his as he helped her over the fence, and for a moment, he was transported back to a time when holding her hand was normal. It took all his willpower not to pull her into his arms and kiss her until her toes curled.

Abbie pulled free the second both her feet were firmly planted. "Let's hurry." He instantly felt the absence of her touch. How he'd taken such a simple thing for granted.

"How'd you hear about this?" he asked. It seemed odd no one had contacted him about such an important thing.

"I have my sources."

Six chutes stood in a row, the metal bars painted a fresh coat of red. They shone in the glimmer of fading sunlight. Wooden plaques were fastened to the gates of four of the chutes, names etched in each.

"Starlight Legends is what the owner called them."

He traced the etched letters that spelled out his dad's name. The pain twisted his heart in a flash. Though he attributed every ride to his dad and thought about him constantly, the loss hit him most here. "He'd hate this, you know. He had no more time for the limelight than I do. He didn't do it for the glory. He did it for himself. To prove to himself that he could."

From the corner of his eye, he saw Abbie fold her arms across her chest. The satchel swung with her shuffling feet.

He stiffened. "You bring me here to talk more about that article?"

"I was hoping you *might* tell me a little more." She met his gaze with gentle eyes. "But no, I wanted you to know. I didn't want you to be surprised."

Though they'd been kids, and only friends back then, she was there when his dad got sick. Eleven miserable days in the ICU, never really sure what each day would bring. It'd been a rollercoaster of hope and despair. She stopped by the hospital every day and brought him something to eat. Stayed until he finished. She knew the extent of his pain when they had to make the decision to move his dad to comfort care.

"Thanks, Abbs." He sniffed back a threatening tear. How many times had he reached for his phone to call his dad and ask for advice before a ride? It'd been more often these last two years. How did you beat a bull who nearly killed you if you never drew him? That was the question he yearned to ask most.

"I didn't want you to be caught off guard by it later. They haven't told anyone about the Starlight Legends. It'll be announced tomorrow night."

She might hate that he was still a bull rider, but she still cared about him. Still knew what might throw him off his game. He wanted to pull her into his arms and hug her tight in thanks. Instead, he shoved his hands into his pockets.

"I have a hundred-acre property," he said in offering. "A few miles outside of Albany. That's my home base." He waited for the realization to register in Abbie's eyes. She slipped a notebook out of her satchel. "It's kind of a mixture of things, but mostly it's a ranch. I have someone who runs things since I'm gone so much of the year. But I have some cattle, half a dozen horses, lots of fun toys." He winked at her, winning a smile.

"Dog?" she asked.

"Pushing your luck, huh?" he teased. "No, no dog." He wasn't home enough. He couldn't fathom owning a dog he paid someone else to care for all the time. But the question reminded him he needed to get Gus to the vet in the morning. "No miniature ponies like you got, either."

"Gibbs isn't a—"

They were interrupted by a loud siren and flashing blue lights. His heart raced a little, but he wasn't about to let Abbie know how much it rattled him. "Looks like it's time to go."

"I knew it!" Abbie shoved her notebook back in her satchel and marched out of the arena. "Logan, this was a bad idea. I can't believe I let you talk me into this. You know how much trouble I could get in if I get arrested?"

"Abbs, relax. You're not—"

"Vince will have my hide!"

He recalled the sheriff he'd seen parked near the town mart, and his breathing went rigid. That old guy hated him. He'd probably be delighted to cast a shadow on Logan's popularity. "Don't worry, I'll take the blame." His sponsors wouldn't be too impressed if he did end up arrested, even for something as harmless as this.

"Let's go." She yanked at his elbow and pulled him a few steps forward. It seemed it only took her a few moments to realize what she'd done, and she dropped her hand. The slightest physical contact between them caused instant sparks neither could deny. "Hurry up."

He stumbled a couple steps before he caught up. Unbelievable how easy it was to fall back into old habits. He hopped the fence first, helping her over as a silhouette emerged from the headlights of a patrol car.

"Hands where I can see 'em," he heard the sheriff call over a megaphone.

He lifted his hands, squinting at the shadow walking their way. The sheriff looked a little lighter on his feet. Quicker, thinner. *Taller?* "Evening, Sheriff," he said. "We didn't mean any harm."

"Hold it," he called when Logan took a step forward. He really hated how bright the glare was against his eyes. Wished he could turn in the opposite direction without raising an alarm.

"Sheriff, it's Logan Attwood, sir."

There was a beat of relief when the flashlight lowered and the man holding it blocked some of the headlight beam with his body. "Logan? Abbie?" Then he started laughing. It didn't sound at all like the man who used to get a kick out of busting him and his friends when they were up to mischief. He couldn't remember the sheriff ever laughing.

"Please don't arrest me," Abbie pleaded.

"Don't worry, Abbs," the sheriff said. "You're not going to jail tonight."

"Cliff?" How Logan hadn't placed his voice immediately was a mystery.

A closer, squinted look at the vehicle and its flashing lights revealed the word *Security* on its side. Not *Sheriff* as Logan had feared.

"You two can't be breaking in here." Cliff walked back to the car and turned off the lights, giving Logan's eyes instant relief. Now all that lit up the grounds was the moonlight. "They have cameras now, you know."

"I tried telling him," Abbie grumbled.

"You're lucky I hadn't called it in yet, or the sheriff would be over here already."

"Cliff, what are you doing out here?" Logan asked.

"Working."

Abbie took a few steps closer to her brother. "Why?"

"Some extra cash, that's all."

Logan tried to follow what might be transpiring between Abbie and her brother, but it wasn't something he could quite put his finger on. If his buddy needed extra money, why hadn't he just asked? He had more than he knew what to do with, plenty to help Cliff's family out. He would've given him some in a heartbeat, no questions asked.

"They already upped your hours at the store," Abbie said. "Why would you want *another* job?"

"Abbie, don't worry about it. Worry about what you and Logan were doing *trespassing*."

"I was just showing Logan the plaque." Abbie marched to her car and yanked open the door. "For his dad."

"You weren't supposed to say anything to anyone."

"You knew, too?" Logan turned to ask his friend

as they watched Abbie speed away. "Cliff, were you going to tell me?"

"I'm sorry, man. I couldn't. New owner wanted it kept under wraps. Telling you might've cost me this job."

Now that Abbie was gone, he felt a little more comfortable offering help. He almost said as much, but found the right words seemed out of reach. Flashes of his grandpa refusing him replayed in his mind. He'd already ruined one relationship; he couldn't risk destroying another.

Somehow, he'd find a discreet way to help Cliff and his family. It was the least he could do for all the times they let him stay with them over the years. "It's all good. Abbie tipped me off, but I won't say anything."

"I have to say, I'm a little surprised to see you two spending so much time together." Was it simply curiosity? Cliff's tone was neutral, impossible to read. Or was there a warning there?

"Yeah, me, too." He shuffled his feet. "It's complicated."

Nothing had ever been simple about Abbie Bennington, except the way he felt about her.

 bbie

"C'mon, Gibbs." Abbie stood holding the door open at the local vet clinic. Her behemoth of a dog had firmly planted his bottom on the ground, making himself as unmovable as the sidewalk.

Despite his hefty size, Gibbs was usually an easy-going dog—except when a trip to the vet was involved. "They have treats inside." Gibbs gave her a side glance that spoke of mild interest, but nothing to promise he could be persuaded with mere dental chews.

Abbie muttered under her breath, wishing she'd brought her mom along. She wasn't sure what she put in those homemade peanut butter treats, but it was surely something magic. She could use their miracle-working abilities right about now.

"I'll let you sleep on the couch whenever you want," she tried again, but Gibbs didn't move. Probably had no clue what luxury she offered him, if his indifferent groan was any indication.

Letting the door fall closed, she tried another tactic. Crouching behind her dog, she shoved with all her might. Though the effort felt a little like moving a concrete barrier, she did manage to nudge him to all fours. Before Gibbs could plop down on her again, she straddled him. Both arms wrapped around his large frame, and with her entire body, she encouraged him toward the door.

She had only a brief moment to consider how embarrassing a sight she must've been when she heard that deep, rumbling laugh behind her. Heat rushed to her cheeks, but she couldn't stop her forward progress. If Gibbs quit shuffling his feet, they might not move again.

"Allow me to get the door."

Resisting the urge to fire a retort, she shoved Gibbs toward the entrance. If she said something stupid, she might lose the help she was lucky enough to happen on. Even if it was from Logan.

The furry bear put up quite the fight, but between the two of them, they managed to contain stray legs when his paws pushed against the door frame, and ushered him inside before he could make any real escape attempt.

"I've heard about dogs not liking the vet, but this is something else." Logan chuckled, that twinkle in his eye causing her heart to skip a couple beats.

She hated to admit how much she'd missed it. How much she had started to look forward to seeing it. *He'll be gone at the end of the week.*

"I think it'll be house calls after this." She checked them in, then managed by some miracle to convince Gibbs to follow her to a seat in the corner. It didn't stop him from trying to crawl into the chair with her. She relented, and hugged the upper half he dropped in her lap. He wore the most pitiful look she'd ever seen.

It hadn't occurred to her to ask why Logan was here. Or why he didn't follow her to a seat. Her nerves tingled with a mixture of realization and terror at how easily they fell back into completely normal moments. If only he wouldn't leave this time, maybe they'd have a real chance. But Logan giving up the rodeo to stay with her was as impossible as roping the moon.

"I'll bring him in." Logan nodded in response to something the receptionist had said to him, then turned toward the door. She could only assume he'd picked up Gus, and wondered how much extra tension the kind gesture caused between him and his grandpa. Gerald worked long days between the auto body shop and the cement factory and likely didn't even know his dog was gone for a checkup.

A few minutes later, Logan reappeared. Her eyes traveled immediately to the floor in search of Gus, but she didn't see him until she lifted her gaze to Logan's arms.

Fear clutched her chest. She'd noticed Gus becoming more lethargic, but this was something more. Unlike Gibbs, Gus was usually excited to come to the vet. But his enthusiasm was limited now to a couple weak tail wags.

"What's wrong with Gus?" she asked Logan when he took a seat across from her.

The twinkle in his eyes from before was gone now, replaced with concern. "Not sure, but whatever it is, I think he might be in pain. He only gets up when he absolutely has to." Logan let out a defeated sigh. "I'm just hoping it's something they can take care of."

She hoped so, too, but words lodged in her throat. Memories of Gus joining them on adventures in the country flashed through her mind. The once energetic, happy dog seemed gone, and a stranger in his place. "How old is he now?"

"Suppose he's about twelve or thirteen."

Old. But not *that* old. She hugged Gibbs tighter. They'd been a part of each other's lives just short of a year, but she couldn't imagine what life would become without him.

Logan stroked the sleepy shepherd in his lap. It appeared Gus had lost a little weight too. "What's Gibbs in for?" Logan asked.

"Just a checkup and a couple shots." Before she could ask what he might do if Gus needed an operation, the receptionist called Gibbs's name.

Removing the clinging dog from her lap, she managed to get to her feet. "Let me know about Gus, okay?"

Logan nodded, trying to smile but failing. Against all rational thought when it came to keeping her distance, she set a hand on his shoulder. "It'll be okay. Let me know if you need anything."

Gibbs didn't give either of them a chance for more as he bolted for the front door when it opened, taking her with him via her grip on his leash. Minor chaos erupted, but with the help of the receptionist, she managed to wrestle the dog into an exam room.

After more than a dozen different treats and a collaborative effort from two assistants and the doctor, Abbie let Gibbs race out the front door. His tail whipped around in excitement with his newfound freedom as they headed to her car. One that would need to be upgraded before too long; Gibbs wouldn't fit in the back seat come Christmas.

Her eyes scanned the parking lot, but there was no sign of Logan's truck. Fear clawed at her chest as she dug her phone out of her purse. The first instinct was to send him a text, and her fingers tapped out half a message before she stopped herself.

He'd reach out when he was ready to talk. If something bad had happened, he would need space.

She'd managed to shuffle Gibbs in the back seat and roll down the windows before her phone buzzed in her hand. She nearly fumbled it under her seat, but her fingers clutched at the edges and saved it from the abyss.

Vince: I want to see a draft of your article.
Vince: Tonight.

She speed-typed a reply saying she had until Sunday and didn't need to be micro-managed, but she deleted it. Seemed text messages were her enemy this morning. Without censoring herself, she might've lost it and said a few things she couldn't take back later, when her emotions were no longer at their height. It was something she'd never been good at, but she was trying lately.

"Looks serious." Logan leaned folded arms in her open window.

"Are you part ninja, too?" She hadn't heard anyone approach. Hadn't even caught that wafting of cologne on the breeze until now. She spied a wicker basket at his side. "What's that?"

He lifted the basket covered with a horse-patterned dish towel that looked suspiciously like one from Erin's kitchen. "A picnic."

"You brought a picnic basket to a vet clinic?"

"There's a park a block over."

She followed his eyes down the street, wanting to be upset about this park's location. But she *was* hungry. "What about Gus?"

"They're running some bloodwork. They want to keep him a while for observation. Not much I can do until they call." He reached out a hand to pet an eager Gibbs and earned a big lick on the arm. "What do you say? Keep a guy company while he waits?"

Her phone buzzed again, but she shoved it in her pocket. Talking to Vince right now was a bad idea. She would write a great article, if only he gave her the space to do it.

"Vince?"

"That obvious?"

"If you'd rather go into the office than eat with me, I won't stop you. But I won't be saving you one of Erin's raspberry scones." That smirk had always been her greatest weakness when it came to Logan Attwood.

Her stomach rumbled. Erin's scones could be used as currency in desperate times, they were that good. "If I come, I'll be working on the interview," she warned. Maybe she wanted him to tell her no. If so, she'd run far in the other direction and save herself. Heartache would surely follow at the end of the week if things kept up like this between them.

"Okay."

Abbie was taken aback at how easy that response came but wasn't about to say anything that might change his mind.

Once Gibbs was on his leash, the trio made their way to the park. Without much luck, she scouted the area for a picnic table that didn't promise splinters. "Maybe I should write a story about this sad little park," she said. "Could convince the community to come together and spruce it up."

"I didn't bring a blanket because I was cold," Logan teased. He led them to a shaded spot beneath a large tree. Before he could smooth out all the corners, Gibbs plopped down in the center and rolled onto his back, causing them both to laugh.

As she joined them on the blanket, her phone buzzed again.

"I'll talk to you about this interview"—Logan stretched out his legs and busied his hands with unpacking the basket of goodies Erin had gathered. Did she see orange juice?—"but you need to talk to your uncle about writing *your* stories."

"It's not that simple, Logan."

"Sure, it is." He poured her a Solo cup of OJ and

handed it over once she was settled. "You can't just wait for him to retire. That could be years away."

Though she didn't want to believe it, she couldn't imagine Vince stepping down in the next decade. That didn't mean he couldn't gradually hand over *some* responsibility. But Logan made a valid point. She wasn't willing to wait ten years to write the kind of stories that mattered most to her. "Okay, I'll talk to him."

"When?"

"Next week."

Logan shook his head. "Not soon enough."

"I need to finish this interview first." Vince wouldn't listen to her at all if her primary assignment wasn't complete and shiny. Even then, chances were slim.

"But you want to put the horse camp story in next week's paper, right?"

Crap. There was that. "Yeah." She wasn't going to admit her plan to sneak it on page fourteen. Though it belonged much closer to the front, her uncle was less likely to pitch a fit if the story ended up that far back and wasn't taking up ad space. Still, he looked over every detail. He'd spot it, of course, and remove it.

"Abbs." Warning hung in his tone, and she knew she'd been caught. Logan held a scone captive until she relented.

"Fine. I'll talk to him sooner." Her phone buzzed

again, causing her to yank it from her pocket so roughly that it flew into the grass on the other side of Logan.

"You always had an arm on you," he said, that twinkle back in his eyes.

Her gaze dropped to his lips, startling her. She couldn't let that kind of thought in. Kissing Logan would solve nothing. It didn't make her want to do it any less, though. "Can I have my phone, please?"

It buzzed again in his hand. "Christy's calling you."

"What?" She snatched the phone from his palm seconds before Gibbs lunged forward, convinced they were all playing a game of keep-away. Logan wrestled with him while she answered the call.

"Abbie! I've been trying to get 'hold of you."

"Is everything okay?" Though she and Christy were not as close of friends as she was with Erin, they did grab lunch a couple times a month, and talked about a mutual love of their favorite TV show, *NCIS*, way more than two sane women should.

"I shouldn't be telling you this."

"What?"

"Your house. It has multiple offers."

Her heart sank into the pit of her stomach. She'd known it was inevitable, that someone would see the value of that big, beautiful Victorian wonder. But secretly she hoped it would sit for a month or more and force the seller to reduce the price somewhere closer to her range. "Thanks for letting me know."

Her despondency must have shown on her face. Logan reached for her hand, squeezing her fingers gently. Compassion filled those dreamy eyes. She'd miss them so much when he left. Didn't want to think about next week when they'd be gone again.

"Do you want to write one?" Christy asked, pulling her from her thoughts.

"Write what?"

"An offer."

She sat up a little straighter. Her scone bounced off her knees, and Gibbs snatched it up in one bite before she or Logan could stop him. "I thought you said I couldn't afford that house." She shook her hand free and ignored the raised eyebrow he gave her.

"You can't," Christy said.

"I don't understand."

"There're three other offers already, and let me be clear that I don't think you'll get the house. *But* you could always write a letter. Let the seller know how much that house means to you. I thought you might regret it if you didn't at least try."

A letter? She couldn't fathom writing a letter to the same woman who'd chased her away with a broom. Somehow, she doubted the seller would find that little tale amusing. She wanted to feel more optimistic about this turn of events, but all she really felt was a twisted knot in her stomach. "When do I have to decide?"

"All offers have to be in by six tonight. Abbie, it's a long shot, and I don't want to get your hopes up."

"I'll think about it, okay?"

"Okay. Call me when you make up your mind. I can email you the paperwork for electronic signatures if that's easier than meeting up today."

"Good. Yeah. Thanks, Christy."

Logan gave her a solid minute after the phone call ended before he pressed. "House?"

"It's nothing."

"Abbs—"

"Ugh!" Before she could successfully turn her phone off or at least on silent and put it face down on the blanket, another text buzzed through. "I have to go. Vince wants us for a team meeting."

ogan

Gibbs made a mad dash for Judith's front counter when Logan arrived with Abbie at the saddlery. He wasn't sure what Judith put in those homemade peanut butter treats, but whatever the secret ingredient was, that dog was addicted.

"Thank you for watching him, Mom," Abbie said. "Carl sneezes nonstop if he gets within twenty feet of Gibbs."

"Everything okay?" Judith asked as she dug out a couple of treats.

Logan tried his best to linger in the background, browsing a rack of button-up shirts while he let the women talk. But his attention was locked on what Abbie might confess. He wanted to know about that house. He wasn't sure whether there was anything he could do, but it was important to her. That much he could tell.

"Besides Vince hounding me to show him a sample of my article?"

Judith lifted the lid off a jar filled with chocolate mints marked at twenty-five cents and handed a couple to Abbie. "Sounds like my brother. Abbs, I know Vince means well. But he needs to give you a chance. Give you space to make your own mistakes."

"Yeah."

"You want me to talk to him?"

Abbie glanced over her shoulder at him across the showroom, catching his eye for a moment. Resolve seemed to settle in hers. "No, don't do that. I'll talk to him after the meeting."

Good. She needed to stand up for herself. His Abbie wasn't usually afraid to do that, but with family, it was more complicated. Especially when her dream was on the line.

Judith lifted her chin, looking at him now. "Those are thirty-percent off this week," she said, a cue to leave the ladies to their conversation if ever he'd been given one. Maybe she thought Abbie was out of sorts because of him.

"Mind if I try one on?" he asked, hoping the compromise would satisfy them both.

"You know the way to the dressing room."

Gibbs, convinced the treats had run out for the moment, trotted down the hall after him. Between the muffled dressing room in the back of the store and Gibbs's heavy panting, it was much harder to hear snippets of their conversation. In fact, it was nearly impossible. He quickly changed shirts, hoping to ask their opinion in order to successfully eavesdrop a little more.

At the end of the hall, he paused, hoping Gibbs wouldn't do anything to give him away. The dog looked at him expectantly, as if there might be some game to be played and he wanted to know the rules.

"Abbie, I wish there was something we could do to help you get that house."

"No, Mom, it's okay. I'm not asking for a loan or anything."

But is she?

"Write the most heartfelt letter you can and hope for the best, sweetie. Have faith that if the house is meant to be yours, it will be."

"If only Mrs. Hampton didn't think I was such a pesky kid." Abbie laughed a pitiful laugh that rang of strength despite the pain in her voice. "Well, I guess I'm going for it, then. I'll text Christy and tell her to send over the paperwork."

Mrs. Hampton. Now he knew which house it was. No question about it, she'd always had her eye on that Victorian home on the edge of town. They'd spent nights lying on a pile of blankets in the bed of his truck stargazing and talking dreamily about living in that house one day. The house and its historic appeal had Abbie's heart. But the property itself with the acreage and horse corral had always snagged his interest.

An image of them living there played out in his head. Abbie curled up on a cushioned wicker chair on the porch writing an article, Gibbs snoozing at her feet, Logan kissing her on the cheek before he went to work with the horses.

He'd been thinking about the future a lot lately. Last night he hardly slept. He wouldn't ride bulls forever. In all likelihood, he wouldn't ride them after this season was over. Either he'd draw Tornado by the finals, or the bull would be retired.

It was what came after that that used to scare him. The year he had off after Tornado nearly killed him had left him feeling lost. He'd never known anything other than bull riding. But after that day at the Andersons' horse camp, he found himself reminiscing about his childhood and how great it'd be to be a part of something like that.

Izzy's question about bull-riding camp echoed in his mind again.

"There, it's done," he heard Abbie say, drawing him and Gibbs both back to the present.

Gibbs, bored with waiting for a game Logan obviously wasn't going to play, bounded into a display of horse brushes on his way to the women, causing both heads at the front counter to shoot in his direction.

"What do you ladies think? Blue my color?"

He parted ways with Abbie at the door of the *Starlight Gazette*. He considered going in, but he wasn't eager to talk to Vince. The man had hounded him for an interview for weeks before he ever hit town, trying to play the family angle. It was no surprise that Abbie was given the assignment over the other writers. Vince was a smart man, even if he was sometimes bullheaded.

Before he let her disappear inside, Logan reached for her hand to stop her. "Do you need a loan, Abbie?"

"What?"

"For the offer."

Any smiles he'd earned that morning were replaced with fiery daggers in her narrowed eyes. "Don't you dare, Logan. This isn't your problem."

"I just want to help, Abbs."

"You forfeited that right when you left two years ago." She flew inside the door, leaving him alone on the sidewalk amid a light summer breeze and a whirl-wind of thoughts.

———

Abbie

Abbie was fuming as the door closed behind her in the *Gazette's* office. *The nerve.* If Logan had stayed and stuck to the plans they made, they'd be buying that house together. They'd be married and living a real life together. How could he possibly think loaning her money would fix anything?

"Abbie, come join us," Vince called from the conference-slash-break room. A box of donuts from Millie's Bakery sat on the table, but their usual enticement didn't grab her.

Vince's glasses were already resting on top of a legal pad. Not a good sign. Not a good sign at all.

Could this day get any worse?

His steely eyes let her know she was late.

"Was that Logan Attwood outside?" Jamie squeaked with excitement. "Like, really him?"

She took a seat at the table. "Yes, that's him." Maybe being seen with Logan would at least buy her some time on that sample if Vince wouldn't relent. If Logan was talking to her, Vince had to accept she would finish the interview that no one else could get.

"Do you have something for me to read?" Vince asked, deflating all hope that he'd wait to bring this up until the pow-wow was over.

"Not yet." Abbie bit down on the inside of her bottom lip. Her temper had never gotten her anywhere with her uncle except backward. "It's a work in progress."

"Abbie, that's not what I asked for."

Any possibility that they could take this offline diminished. Vince was trying to prove a point, but why he felt the need to do it in front of the most non-confrontational part-timer and a summer intern was beyond her. "I'm going with him to the rodeo tonight. I'll be there when they honor his dad. It'll all be part of the article."

"Then I'll expect something first thing in the morning." Vince reached for his glasses and slid them back on, leaving them at the tip of his nose.

She waited through assignment check-ups from both Carl and Jamie for the team meeting to adjourn, then followed Vince into his office. It was quite clear by the door nearly closed in her face that he was done with their discussion.

"What is it?"

She had to make a choice: stand her ground about submitting a full article on Sunday when it was due or beg for him to print the story about the Andersons' horse camp. The odds that she could get him to do both seemed dismal.

"I wanted to talk to you about a story I put together." Someday she might have the power to slip stories in without him knowing until it was too late. But for now, he combed every inch of the paper before it went to print.

"We've already discussed the story you're writing. It's your only priority this week."

"And it will be done. On time." She bit back the urge to tell him how lucky it was for the paper that Logan agreed at all, even if she was a little peeved at him for interfering in her life. He *was* entitled to his privacy if that's what he wanted. "I want to discuss a different one, for the back section. It's already written. An article about the Andersons' horse camp."

Vince let out a heavy sigh as he dropped into his cushioned office chair. "We already discussed this. It's not a newsworthy story people want to read."

"It's exactly the kind of story people want to read." She tensed. Why did these things always mean going to battle with her uncle? "It's a feel-good story about overcoming obstacles and creating something wonderful. Their ranch was going into foreclosure, but they saved it by turning it into what it is today. They create memories for the kids who go there. I even have testimonials."

Vince looked at her as if to ask, *You done?* "No."

Her fists balled at her sides as she tried—oh, she tried—to take a couple deep breaths and calm down. But inside, her temper raged. "Is this because they didn't buy an ad?"

"Of course not." But he wouldn't meet her eyes.

"I understand ads are important to the bottom line, but—"

"I don't think you do understand, Abigail. You

know nothing about the financials of running a news-paper office."

It took everything in her not to shout at Vince, because she very much wanted to yell, *You won't teach me!* But she knew she'd only sound like a little kid throwing a tantrum.

"This story runs next week, or there won't be an exclusive interview with Logan Attwood." She wasn't sure where the words came from. Though it was her voice, they felt much too brave and daring. She feared he would call her bluff, but deep down, she wasn't sure she *was* bluffing.

Vince folded his hands in his lap, his lips pressed in a straight line as he leaned back in his chair and tried to level her with his stern stare. "If you don't submit the first five hundred words by 9 a.m. tomor-row, I'll consider that your formal resignation."

"All I've ever wanted to write are stories like Grandma used to. She'd print this one in a heart-beat. She'd understand how much it would touch the lives of the readers to know something so wonderful exists in our community." She had to take breath because that had all come out at once in a jumble. "It's not all about money or the juiciest story. It's about hope."

Vince threw his glasses onto his desk, his face and neck turning a shade of red she rarely saw. "I'll be deducting the photography fee for that unautho-rized story from your next paycheck."

"You're really *that* opposed to printing the horse camp story?"

"I've already given you my decision."

She stormed out of his office, swiped her purse and the lone framed picture of her and Gibbs off her desk. The rest she didn't need.

She returned to the threshold of Vince's office long enough to say, "Then consider this my formal resignation. I quit."

 ogan

Earlier that morning, when Logan had stopped by his grandpa's place to pick up Gus, he found the front door unlocked. In Starlight, it wasn't uncommon for folks to do that. But it was unusual for Grandpa, who'd harped on him growing up to make sure the front door was locked if he was the last one leaving the premises.

He'd tried calling Grandpa once since his last visit, but his voicemail box was full. He didn't feel entirely guilty swiping the final notice letter from the cluttered kitchen table. Nor did he feel too guilty about the lawn service he'd hired to spruce up the overgrown yard and excess of weeds, or the roofer scheduled to come out tomorrow morning to replace the missing shingles.

If his grandpa wouldn't accept his money and instead insisted on working himself to the bone with two jobs, Logan didn't care if the older man got upset with him for the rest of it.

Taking Gus to the vet had been the priority, of course, but the notice was next on his list.

He entered the big brick bank on the corner of Main and Fourth. The building was original, built back at the turn of the twentieth century, a detail he only knew because of Abbie and her love of old buildings.

He'd gone on a couple of dates more than a year after he left Starlight, but those women didn't hold any appeal to him. Abbie was smart, ambitious, and passionate. She could hold a grudge, but she had a kind, generous heart—all qualities he'd failed to find in another.

He hoped she'd forgive him for offering her a loan. Come around to understand he was only trying to help. If he had stayed, maybe they'd be buying that house together and the money wouldn't be an issue.

As he waited in the bank line, he wondered about the house. When they were younger, he went with her one time to peek in the windows. How they hadn't gotten caught was only dumb luck. Mrs.

Hampton had stood on the porch, shouting and waving her broom because she knew someone was out there. They'd been saved by the lilac bushes.

"Logan Attwood," a teller greeted him, stars in her eyes.

"I need—"

"Do you want something to drink? Water, coffee, tea?"

He glanced at the other open counter and noticed the customer there was not sipping on any sort of beverage. Sometimes he really missed being just another guy who nobody recognized. But with the career he had, that guy was a distant memory. "No, thanks."

"What can I do for you today?" she managed to get out around a too-wide smile.

He pulled a folded envelope from his shirt pocket and slid that along with a check he'd filled out first thing this morning across the counter. "I'd like to pay that in full, please."

The teller tried a couple of times to say something more, but her words kept getting tangled in her throat. She excused herself to talk to her manager.

He would slip back to Grandpa's after this errand and put the notice right back where it had been buried, along with a note about Gus. Though everything else he lined up would be glaringly obvious, settling this debt would be more subtle; there was no need to tell his grandpa. The man would figure it out sooner or later. Hopefully, Logan would be hundreds of miles away at an event when that happened.

Grandpa Gerald had always had an issue with pride, and a temper to go with it. But Logan didn't care. No one should be forced to work two jobs and still be backed into a corner to sell their home. He'd risk upsetting Grandpa indefinitely if it meant giving the man options.

A thin man with thick-rimmed glasses returned with the smiling teller. Logan recognized the man, but couldn't recall his name. He'd helped Logan set up his first checking account, though.

"Is there a problem?" he asked. "The check is good. You can verify that on your computer there. I still bank here, you know."

"No problem at all. Just an unusual circumstance."

Sure, his name wasn't on Grampa's account, but why would the bank care *who* the funds came from as long as they received their money?

The thin man slipped behind the computer screen and his fingers scrambled over the keys. A moment later, he looked up. "Everything is good. Do you need a receipt, Mr. Attwood?"

"Please."

The man slid him the printout and he folded it into his wallet. Now there was only one task left on his to-do list: Track down Abbie's realtor.

Abbie

Abbie's entire body shook. "What have I done?" Any sane person would've left the office without quitting, and at least given it some serious thought overnight before making a completely rash life decision. Though, it'd felt wonderful to let out years of frustration.

After holing up in the back office of the saddlery to pen an imploring, heartfelt letter to Mrs. Hampton, she collected Gibbs and slipped out the door while her mom assisted a customer. She yearned for home, even if home was only a guest cottage in her brother's back yard. At least it was hers.

Gibbs had made it halfway across the back yard when he jolted to a halt and altered course ninety degrees.

"Should've known I'd find you out here," she told Logan. She wanted to stay mad at him for offering her that loan, but she didn't have the energy left. And he didn't deserve that, she'd come to realize. While writing that letter, her anger had softened. He was only trying to help, in the only way he knew how.

He sat by the fire pit, pushing around the cold

ashes. It was much too early in the day to light a fire for no reason. "Everything okay, Abbs?"

"Why did you go back, Logan?"

He stared at the fire pit for a few moments before he lifted his gaze to her. "Have to beat Tornado."

She shivered. She'd never forget that bull or the way he stomped on Logan. Those sharp horns, that crazy look in his eyes. She'd tried to get Tornado pulled from the rodeo circuit after Logan had been in intensive care for two weeks, but no one would listen to her.

"Why? He almost *killed* you."

"Something my dad told me."

She stopped herself from interrupting. He had been very close with his dad growing up, but he rarely talked about him. Even now, more than a decade later, it was a painful topic.

"He told me, 'Never let a bull best you.'" Logan set down the stick. "They retire him after this season. See? I'm running out of opportunities."

She wanted to understand, she really did. But it didn't make sense. A dozen questions danced on the tip of her tongue, but all of them would cause an argument. Instead, she let out a heavy sigh, dropped into a lawn chair, and leaned back in defeat.

"You sure everything is okay?" he asked.

Though every instinct told her to keep her mouth shut, to keep Logan as far from her problems as possible, she broke with one solitary glance at those dark, sympathetic eyes. "I think I just quit my job."

Those eyes widened. "You what?"

Gibbs came back to her side. That magical ball of fur always seemed to know when she needed to squeeze him tight. He tried to crawl in her lap but failed. Still, he managed a lick to her cheek before he hopped down. "Vince won't print the horse camp story. Flat-out refuses."

"So, naturally you had to quit?"

She shrugged. It hadn't been until that heated moment with her uncle that she realized how much leverage she had. Still, she hadn't expected things to go so south. "Good news is you're off the hook for the interview."

He didn't say anything to that, and his silence caused her to look over. She couldn't read that blank expression, but something important was going through his mind. He asked, "What're you going to do?"

"I'll figure something out." She laced her fingers around her knees. "I have some money saved up, and Cliff'll let me stay here until I get it all sorted out." She'd been tempted to tell Christy to pull her offer, but the chances of it being accepted were so dismal she didn't see the point of another text. Mrs. Hampton would never be won over with an offer fifty-thousand low. She wasn't exactly known to be the sympathetic type, especially about an offer with some silly letter from a girl with a childhood dream of living there.

"You could start your own paper," Logan suggested.

"What?"

"Yeah. Write your own. See which one really does better."

She shook her head. "Even if I had the money, which I definitely do not, I'd never do that. Vince is family. My grandma would hate it." Grandma would hate seeing all this animosity happening now. "Maybe it's time to face reality. Find another dream to chase."

Tears threatened the corners of her eyes. She'd never had another dream.

"Abbs." She hadn't noticed him standing, much less walking over to her. But she didn't fight him when he pulled her to her feet and wrapped her in his arms. "Everything will be okay. You'll see."

"I don't know, Logan."

He kissed the top of her forehead. "You can't give up on your dream. I won't allow it."

Despite the world falling apart around her, she felt calm in his embrace. Protected. She'd missed this feeling so much. "Logan, I—" The mistake had already been made, tilting her head back and daring to look in those smoldering eyes.

With a gentleness a bull rider should never have, he traced his fingers along her cheek and trailed them down her neck. Such strong emotion swam in their shared gaze. Happiness, hurt, joy, anger. Love.

She could lie to herself all she wanted, but her heart knew better. It would always belong to Logan Attwood, no matter how far away he went.

He tipped her chin up, and slowly brought his lips to hers. He gave her the chance to break free and run, as she should. It was the only way to protect her heart from shattering. But she was helpless to do anything but await his kiss.

Finally, his lips met hers. Softly. Reminiscent.

He trailed a few kisses along her cheek to her ear, stopping to whisper, "I'll always love you, Abbs. Always." The next kiss made her dizzy. Her fingers tingled as they wrapped their way around the back of his neck and combed through his hair. She didn't know what any of this meant, but it felt like hope.

ogan

"We're at the rodeo!" Izzy's feet bounced against her booster seat in Cliff's truck. The excitement in those blue eyes was as pure as Logan'd ever seen it. It made him smile, and Abbie, too. Then they smiled at each other. She must've noticed the heat in his gaze, because pink crept onto those soft cheeks.

The memory of that kiss had them both a little dizzy, it seemed. But they had yet to talk about what it meant.

"She's been going crazy all day," Erin said about Izzy. "I thought she was excited for horse camp, but this is something else. I think *someone* told her some stories about the rodeo." Her pointed stare was aimed at him, but a smile spread on her face.

He wondered if Abbie had told anyone about that kiss—mostly whether she'd told Erin.

"It's not too late to sign her up for the mutton busting," he said. "I think she'd have a blast."

"No!" Erin said. "I'm not putting my daughter on the back of some wild sheep."

"Pleeeeease!" Little legs bounced with even more vigor than before. "I *want* to ride a sheep."

"Oh, come on," Abbie said. "Izzy is fearless. Besides, she has to wear a helmet."

"She could get *hurt*." Erin aimed that narrowed stare at him. He had to assume Abbie had *not* said anything about that kiss or she might be acting a whole lot differently right now—more like excluding him completely from the conversation.

"Can't keep her in a bubble all her life, you know." Cliff reached across the center console and squeezed his wife's hand. Erin wriggled it free. If only she or Abbie knew that Izzy's name was already on the list and a cute purple helmet was packed in a bag on the back seat.

"The sheep are shorter than Gibbs," he dared. He didn't elaborate that it was a shorter distance to fall. Besides, they'd already put Izzy on Gibbs a couple times while Erin was running errands, to help her get the hang of how to hold on. The dog had loved it, too. "Kids do it all the time."

"Pleeeease!" Izzy continued.

Erin let out a heavy sigh. "I'll think about it."

Cliff pulled into the VIP lot, courtesy of Logan's competitor package. There were perks to his fame, he had to admit, after they passed the already-full general admission parking lot. Anyone who hadn't arrived yet would be forced to pay for parking from those selling space around town. It felt good to use his status to do something nice for his friends.

It was a little surreal after all this time to be walking toward the arena with Abbie by his side. For two years, he'd gone to all these events alone. Checked his phone every time to see if maybe she'd texted him a *Miss you* or *Good luck*. But it was always the same: silence.

"You did it?" he overheard Erin say to Abbie, and his ears perked. "You really put in an offer?"

"I'm not going to get it," Abbie told her, the excitement dimming in her eyes. He yearned to reach for her hand, but that could cause a whole new set of problems right now in front of Erin and Cliff. One amazing kiss didn't mean they had anything sorted out. "But Christy thought I should at least put my name in the hat."

Guilt crept in at what he'd done, but he couldn't imagine that house going to anyone else. He genuinely hoped Mrs. Hampton would read Abbie's letter and forget all the other offers on the table, but he doubted it would play out like that.

"Must feel good to be back," Cliff said, pulling him from eavesdropping on Abbie's conversation. "Doing what you love in your hometown."

"It does," he said, and he meant it. There'd be more pressure to perform well this weekend with the entire town expecting him to win the event, but he'd always managed to quiet the crowd in his mind while he was atop a bull. He could do it here, too.

After he got everyone inside the gates, Cliff pulled him away to grab food for the group. Reluctantly, he let Abbie walk away toward her seat. Now that he had her back, he didn't much care for being separated. He didn't want a single moment to transpire that might change her mind.

"You think Erin will let Izzy on a sheep?" he asked.

"We'll find out."

If not, that would be another strike against him, he suspected. It'd been his idea, after all.

A couple of fans stopped him for an autograph, and he obliged despite his desire to simply blend in. His sponsors would be happy he was being social, but he had to admit he wouldn't miss this part once he retired.

They ordered a bunch of hot dogs, nachos, and drinks, and carried their haul back to the VIP section of the grandstands where the others waited for them. Another glimpse into the normal life he sacrificed by leaving.

He had to admit, he was rather impressed with the upgrades. This section was much less crowded, the seats had padded backs to them, and there were even stationary tables for their food. "Someone really poured a lot of money into this," he mentioned to Cliff. "They must have high expectations."

"Some guy from California with money to burn, chasing a dream."

Cliff's comment had him considering his own dreams and what might come next, after this season. He was young enough yet. He could ride a couple more years, if it came down to it. Most riders he knew retired in their early thirties. But did he want that?

"Thanks for the nachos," Abbie said, bringing him back to the present moment as he took a seat beside her.

"Of course." That dazzling smile was for him. What would it take to keep it that way indefinitely? "Abbs, maybe we should talk—"

"Oh, look!" She grabbed his arm and pointed toward a sectioned area of the arena where a gaggle of kids were corralled. "They're going to do the greased-pig contest!"

Cliff leaned in with a chuckle, saying to his wife, "Be glad we didn't sign her up for that."

"I hope Carl lined up Jillian to get pictures for—" Abbie stopped herself, her smile fading into a frown.

"I guess I don't need to worry about stuff like that anymore, do I?"

The despair in her tone tore at his heart. He resisted the urge to take her hand in his own, worried he'd draw too much attention when neither were ready for that. "I'm sorry, Abbs," he said quietly. "Just try to enjoy the show. Lotta fun stuff tonight."

He'd like to have a few choice words with Vince, but he wasn't sure it'd do any good. In fact, he'd probably make things worse. Vince, though stubborn, was a mostly reasonable man from what Logan remembered. With time, he might realize the mistake he'd made in letting Abbie walk out the door.

Or he might not.

The latter gave Logan the smallest reassurance that he did the right thing about the house.

Laughter won over when the first little black greased pig was released and the youngest group of kids was set loose. Squeals sounded through the air as the youngsters fell one by one. Izzy's laughter was the loudest, the purest. It seemed to revive Abbie.

Again, he met those eyes. She had to be thinking the same thing. That this time they really could build a life together. Raise a family.

He'd been thinking more and more about what an unknowingly wise five-year-old asked him at horse camp. *Do they have a camp for bull riders too?* At first, he dismissed the idea. Though bull-riding camps did exist, they were few and far between. He had the money to gamble on a business idea, but not a lot extra if one didn't pan out.

Still, a part of him wondered if he could make it work.

Abbie laid a hand on his shoulder, shaking him from his thoughts. The heat of her touch caused his pulse to race. "I think you have to go." She nodded toward the announcer's booth. "Act surprised," she added in a whisper.

Halfway to the announcer's stand for what they told him was just a quick meet-and-greet for the fans, his phone rang.

"I have some great news, Mr. Attwood," Kate Riggs said to him. His new realtor since Christy wasn't willing to get tangled in the middle of such shenanigans—conflict of interest, she deftly told him. "The seller accepted your offer, with one small counter."

A blend of emotions hit him. Excitement that his plan had worked; disappointment that Abbie's letter had not; apprehension that she wouldn't take the news well. "Thanks, Kate. That *is* great news. What's the counter?" But he could barely hear Kate through the blaring speaker, roaring crowd, and squealing pig.

"Sounds like you're busy."

"Rodeo."

"Why don't you stop by in the morning to discuss things, then you can sign the paperwork? You have until tomorrow to respond." She'd offered before to send everything electronically, but he had never trusted a document he couldn't sign in person.

"I'll be by your office first thing." He'd hardly hung up the phone before one of the announcers spotted him and came right over.

He was grateful to Abbie for sneaking him into the arena last night, or the jolt he'd have received from unexpectedly seeing his dad's name etched into the chute door would cripple him. He missed his dad every day, but he missed him most in the arena. Wished he could ask his advice before a ride, discuss what he'd done wrong or where he could improve after an event.

He caught Abbie staring at him from the stands on the other side of the arena and gave her a little wave. She waved back. She'd always known him better than anyone. Better than he knew himself.

bbie

Logan had hardly been gone a full minute before Erin stole his seat next to Abbie. "You mind telling me what all this is about?" she demanded.

Other than Gibbs, who'd been the lone witness, she hadn't told a soul about that kiss. There really hadn't been the chance. But mostly, she wasn't ready to talk about it. With anyone. "What do you mean?" The playing-stupid routine would never work long, if at all, on Erin.

"You two." She waved her hand as if Logan were still sitting there. "You seem like you're getting along —I'm glad you are, for the record—but just curious, what changed? Did that article finally help you two find closure?"

It had been a while since she last saw Erin for more than a few chaotic moments outside of dinners, and a lot had happened. She had decided the family drive to the rodeo was not the best time to tell her sister-in-law how she quit her job earlier that day. "I'm not writing the article anymore."

"Come again?"

Squeals sounded as an older group of kids now chased after a slightly bigger greased pig, but she couldn't focus on that no matter how hard she tried. "I quit." She braced herself with a steadying breath, then relayed the story to Erin as it'd played out that morning—minus the afternoon kiss in the back yard. Her best friend only missed that little scene because she'd been grocery shopping in town.

"Vince'll come around, Abbs."

"You sound pretty sure of that."

"That paper can't survive without you."

"Just for this week, and only because of the one story he won't be able to get without me." She took a long sip of her fountain drink. *Dr. Pepper*. Logan remembered. Her thoughts trailed to that ring stuck beneath her dresser. How did one tell their ex-fiancé that they were thinking about wearing it again? It was such a foolish and rash thought. They'd hardly sorted anything out, and maybe they wouldn't.

Perhaps that ring was stuck under her dresser because it wasn't meant to be worn.

Erin bumped her shoulder. "You look like you've seen a ghost."

She didn't realize she'd let her thoughts wander so carelessly. Around Erin, of all people, it was a dangerous thing to do. "I'm not even sure I want my job back, Erin." There, that ought to keep any possible mention of Logan out of the conversation.

"You'd give up your dream? Just like that? I don't think so."

"I don't *want* to," she said. "But I also don't want to operate strictly under Vince's terms. It's suffocating. He won't budge an inch on anything he doesn't agree on."

The announcer riled up the crowd with the final round of the greased-pig contest, this time for adults. She caught sight of Carl on the sideline with his electronic notepad. Would he get all her assignments now? Unlike everyone else, she wasn't so sure Vince would offer her job back. The man was too proud to do it anytime soon.

"You could work at another paper, if you're willing to move."

"This is home."

"I know it is. And selfishly, I don't want you to leave." Erin dunked a nacho in thick cheese sauce. "You have all the leverage, Abbs. Remember that when he asks you to come back."

"Maybe."

Cliff excused himself, taking a demanding Izzy with him in search of Skittles, leaving Abbie all alone with her best friend.

"Now on to the *real* question," Erin said.

"What?"

Near the chutes, one of the staff members lined up four people, each with a connection to the person their respective chute was being dedicated to. Erin's eyes followed her gaze. "You and Logan. What's the deal?"

"I don't know—"

"Knock it off, Abbs. You two are all but wrapped around each other. All starry eyed, too."

She felt her cheeks heat. "We kissed." There, it was out in the open.

"You what?"

"It just happened, earlier today. I don't know if it even means anything." But oh, it sure seemed like it did. They'd shared many kisses over the years, but this one was different. This one gave her hope, and that terrified her more than anything.

"He's leaving in a few days, Abbs."

That dreaded detail couldn't be escaped, no matter how hard she wanted to ignore it. Logan would leave, no matter how much she might beg him to stay. He had a whole other life in Albany. Other rodeo events to compete in. What if he left this time and never came back? "I know."

"Have you guys *talked* about it?"

She twisted her Styrofoam cup in her hands, desperately trying to avoid Erin's severely inquisitive gaze. "Not yet."

"If you two are going to give it a real shot, I'm all for it. Truly, I am." Erin wrapped an arm around her shoulders and squeezed. "But if he breaks your heart, I'll make sure he never dares to step foot in Starlight again."

"Thanks, Erin."

The grip around her shoulders loosened as a muttered string of words quietly slipped from Erin's disbelieving lips. "Why is my daughter wearing a *helmet*?"

"Guessing Izzy didn't go to find Skittles." She tried to hide her smile at her brother's subterfuge. She'd ridden a sheep as a little girl, too, back in the days that the rodeo still came to Starlight. She'd scraped an elbow, but otherwise competed unscathed.

"I'm going to kill him." Though she expected her friend to fly out of her seat and intercept her daughter before the chute dedication was finished, Erin stayed put. Her fingers clenched the edges of the bleacher.

"Erin, it's a fluffy sheep, running around a pen blanketed in soft dirt."

"Whose side are you on?" But Erin let out a relenting sigh as she watched her daughter and her husband huddle together, probably discussing strategy. "Suppose if I don't let her do this, she'll just talk about it nonstop until I find another rodeo to take her to."

Abbie's eyes danced between Izzy in the adorable little purple helmet as she listened to her dad's advice and Logan by the chutes as the announcer went one by one with the dedications. Someday, Logan's name would be on one of those chutes, too, she suspected.

"You warned him about this, didn't you?" Erin asked, nodding toward Logan.

"Had to."

"You still care, that's why."

"Probably my curse, but yes."

"Still love him?"

Before she was forced into answering, the announcers switched gears and jazzed up the crowd for the mutton busting competition. Erin's hand slapped her arm and held on in a death grip. It'd be amusing if her fingers weren't shackled so tightly.

"Someone stole my seat, I see." Logan had made quick work of escaping the chute area, and the gaggle of fans who no doubt tried to ambush him.

"You're not getting it back," Erin replied, her eyes never leaving her daughter. "I know you were in on this."

"Most kids last less than eight seconds," Logan reassured her, taking another seat. Abbie was admittedly a little sad about the distance, but wasn't brave enough to try to move the nervous mother. "She'll be done before you know it. And I bet she has fun."

The first couple of kids fell off in less than three seconds, and Erin's fingers pressed into her arm even harder, especially when the little girl in the purple helmet exited the chute, arms and legs wrapped around the bouncy sheep.

Unsuccessfully, Erin covered her eyes with her free hand. "I can't watch." But between her daughter and the clock, she couldn't tear her gaze away.

Within the first four seconds, Izzy slid onto the side of her sheep. She held on until eleven seconds lapsed, when she finally plopped onto the freshly turned-up dirt. She was on her feet instantly, bouncing around as the announcer congratulated her stellar performance. Cliff stood smiling on the sideline.

"See, that wasn't so bad," Logan said to Erin. "She's a natural."

"I'll let you know how I feel *after* I inspect her for scrapes and bruises." But Erin didn't sound as bent out of shape now that it was over. In fact, a sliver of a smile appeared to be lurking along those straight-lined lips.

"Mommy, Mommy!" Izzy blazed across the front of the stands and zipped up the steps to Erin. "Did you see? Did you see? I rode a sheep!"

"I thought you were going to get some Skittles," Erin said, directing most of her comment to Cliff.

"That's the sheep!" Pride beamed from that adorable smiling girl at sharing that snippet of knowledge. "Isn't that a cool name?"

"A sheep named Skittles," Logan joined in. "How about that?"

"Well," Erin said, switching spots with Logan so she could sit by her husband, "what did you think, Izzy?"

"It was fun!" Izzy went a hundred miles an hour describing her experience in pieces, always remembering something she'd forgotten. It made Abbie's heart swell, to see such innocent excitement in her niece.

Logan slipped his hand on top of hers beneath the table, leaning closer. "We could still have that, you know. A life together. A family."

"I don't know—"

He squeezed her hand. "Give it a chance, Abbs."

 ogan

"Are you going to marry Aunty Abbie?" Izzy asked Logan at breakfast the next morning. Abbie choked on her coffee. His forkful of French toast froze midair at the innocent but blunt question of an inquiring little girl.

"Honey, finish your eggs." Erin came in for the save. "No more questions until they're gone."

"But—"

"No buts. Finish your eggs."

That idea hadn't left his mind since the day it took root years ago. He *wanted* to marry Abbie. More than once he almost asked if she still had the ring, but hadn't yet been able to brace for the answer. He hoped she kept it, but if she wanted him to, he'd buy another.

"You heard from the vet?" she asked, obviously as eager as him to divert attention. Izzy did tend to bounce from topic to topic, but she was a smart little cookie. She might ask again if something more interesting didn't pop up in conversation.

"Not since yesterday afternoon. Figured I'd check in after breakfast."

The vet hadn't called yet, but Grandpa had. Logan wasn't brave enough to answer. Not until he knew what was wrong with Gus and what could be done. He would pay for it all, but he didn't want Grandpa interfering before all that was sorted out. He'd listen to what was likely a scathing voicemail later.

"Who's Gus?"

"Izzy, eat!"

"But my eggs are gone," she protested.

"Then work on that French toast."

"Gus is my dog," he answered. Because Gus would always be *his* dog. They picked him out together as a family when he was a teenager, but the dog rode home in Logan's lap. Slept at the foot of his bed despite his love of being outside. "He lives with my grandpa now."

Abbie pushed her eggs around with her fork. "I hope he's okay."

"What's wrong with him?"

"He's not feeling well," Logan explained. He hoped whatever was ailing the aging dog could be treated. He wasn't ready to lose him, and despite his grandpa's apparent lack of interest, he doubted he was either.

"Can we get a dog?"

"No."

"You don't need a dog," Abbie said to her. "You can play with Gibbs whenever you want. He needs someone to keep him on his paws."

"He does?"

The chocolate mass perked up from his spot on the floor beside Izzy's seat. He'd had a pretty boring morning as Izzy hadn't managed to drop any scraps yet. He licked the little girl's bare foot, winning a giggle.

"Think you can do that?"

Izzy's eyes locked on Gibbs, as though sizing him up as thoughts buzzed through that busy little mind. "Yeah."

When Abbie's phone rang, everyone looked her way, including the dog. He watched her smile fall into a more serious expression. "It's Christy." Scooting her chair back, she slipped into the hallway off the kitchen.

Guilt twisted inside him, knowing the news she was about to receive. She had her heart set on that house, and knowing his Abbie, she wanted to do it herself. But the low offer along with her current unemployment didn't bode well for her, even if he hadn't interfered.

"You know something." Erin kept her voice low, but the sternness in that tone still managed to give him chills.

He watched the doorway for Abbie's return, hoping it would be soon enough to avoid answering the question. Erin had a way with people that made it nearly impossible to get away with a lie. That Cliff had been able to keep Izzy's sheep ride a secret was a miracle itself.

"You know she won't get it." He hoped to stay as neutral as possible. The last thing he wanted was to tell Erin of all people what he did. He'd rather face Abbie's dad. "Mrs. Hampton doesn't exactly have a soft spot for people and their disadvantages."

Izzy slipped a piece of bacon off her plate and under the table. If Gibbs had been a little quieter inhaling it, she might've gotten away with it. But Erin didn't seem to care at the moment. "I wish you were wrong, but I know you're not."

"Wish I were, too."

"Well?" Erin asked when Abbie reentered the kitchen.

Abbie simply shook her head. Her head dipped down, hair curtaining her grim expression. "I've got a couple things to do," she said, her voice cracking. He recognized her expression; tears would soon follow. "Let me know when the vet calls, okay?"

"Abbs—" But he let her go before she cried in front of them all.

"She didn't have a chance," Erin said when they could see Abbie walking across the back yard toward her cottage. She left so fast Gibbs hadn't even had an opportunity to decide *if* he wanted to go with her. But now the dog abandoned his spot near the table to watch her out the window and whine.

Logan's resolve to keep his secret nearly broke. Maybe telling Erin what he did wouldn't be so bad. It could work in his favor, after she cooled off about the unexpected news. But with Izzy in their company, the secret would never stay secret. "I'll take Gibbs over in a few minutes."

"If you'd stayed like you planned, you'd be buying that house." Erin noisily stacked plates and silverware. *"Together."* She marched to the sink. "Izzy, go wash your hands, please."

Then again, the secret seemed better kept with him. It'd come out in a few days anyway, but for now, he didn't feel like dealing with any grief he might receive. He set the tub of butter in the fridge and left the bottle of syrup on the counter beside the stove.

Erin braced herself on the edge of her farmhouse sink. "I meant what I said the first day you showed up. Don't hurt her, Logan. She acts tough, but you should know better than anyone how fragile she can be."

He did. "I want to make this work," he said. "Not just for this week. For the long haul."

"Good."

Halfway to the front door, he stopped and quickly scanned the area for Izzy before he spoke. If he gave away her birthday surprise, Erin would probably turn him out within ten seconds and force him to sleep in his truck. "I'd like to help."

"What are you talking about?"

"I know why Cliff is working a second job."

"It's just for this week."

Somehow he didn't think it would end after a week. The owner would likely offer him more shifts, especially during events, and Cliff would take them. He knew how expensive keeping some girls happy could be. One week working security, even for some rich Californian, wouldn't be enough.

"Cliff would never accept the money from me," he said. "But maybe you can talk to him. If you let me know how much you need, I'll make it happen."

"Logan, we couldn't possibly accept your money."

"I want do something right for a change. You've been more than kind to let me stay here when you could've forced me to book a hotel room and deal with the mob following me around. Let me help you make your little girl's dream come true."

Erin gave him a gentle, appreciative smile. At least for the moment, he'd won her over. Come Sunday, it might be a different story.

"Gibbs, let's go." The fluffy dog abandoned his lookout post at the window, leaving behind a few nose smudges on the glass. He trotted toward the back door, floppy ears swaying.

The overcast sky suggested a possible morning shower, a heavy one from the looks of it. He'd never been a particular fan of a muddy arena, not since he face-planted in a deep mud puddle his first year on the main circuit. Hopefully, everything would dry up before tonight's event.

Gibbs plopped down outside Abbie's door and waited as he knocked. "Abbs, you there?" The dog tilted his head at some *thunk* from inside. It didn't sound life-threatening, but Logan tried the knob anyway. "Abbie?"

The dog darted through the cottage toward the bedroom in the back. He followed, stopping in the doorway. Abbie sat atop her tall dresser, an arm stretched behind it. A hefty book lay sprawled on the floor, seemingly the culprit of the earlier *thunk*.

Gibbs hopped up on his hind legs, and dang if that dog's nose wasn't an inch from the dresser top. In another month, he'd be able to see the top of it standing like that.

"My arm is stuck."

Logan didn't chuckle at all, just muscled the

piece of furniture a couple inches away from the wall, allowing Abbie to wriggle herself free. She pulled up a yard stick with a ball of masking tape on its end. "Looking for something?" It was covered in lint, but nothing of value he could see.

Abbie let out an exaggerated sigh. "Didn't find it."

"Find what?"

"What I was looking for."

"Which was?"

"Never mind. Help a girl down?"

Lifting her to lower her to the floor, he smiled as her arms wrapped around him without the slightest hesitation. They lingered there, too, as he took the moment to hold her a little closer and kiss her forehead. They'd shared a few kisses after the rodeo last night, and first thing this morning when he came to fetch her for breakfast. But now, he just wanted her to know he was there for her.

"I'm sorry your offer didn't get accepted."

She hugged him a little tighter, nestling her cheek against his chest. "I guess I knew I wouldn't get it. Some people might find it amusing that they used to chase me away from their house with a broom, but Mrs. Hampton just isn't one of them."

"She's a tough one."

"And even if she had picked my offer, where would that leave me? Begging for my job back? No thanks."

As he was about to ask if she'd heard from Vince, his phone vibrated in his shirt pocket. She giggled at the buzzing as it must have tickled, but her expression went solemn when she saw it was the vet calling.

"Guess we better go find out about Gus."

———

"Lyme disease, you're sure?" Logan asked Dr. Charles. They'd been greeted in the waiting area of the vet clinic but had yet to see Gus. With the news, he couldn't help but crane his neck around the receptionist at the front counter, hoping to see into the back exam area.

"Cases in Wyoming are pretty rare compared to many other states," the doctor said, "but they do happen. We ran some tests to confirm."

Abbie squeezed his hand.

He had patted Gus down, looking for any hint of what might be wrong prior to taking him in. It just didn't seem possible that he missed spotting a deer tick.

"Looks like he had a tick but someone didn't get the whole thing pulled out." Dr. Charles folded his arms. "It's the bacteria in those pinchers that causes it." He went on to explain a few more things, how long it'd likely been since Gus acquired the parasite and the treatment plan to follow.

"It *can* be treated?" Abbie asked.

"Yes, it's early enough that I think some antibiotics and an anti-inflammatory should do the trick." The doctor explained what treatment at home would require, and that Gus would be more susceptible in the future.

At the mention of thirty days, Logan's eyes widened. "He needs medication for an entire month?" He couldn't fathom his grandpa giving Gus medication twice a day for a week, much less a whole month. Not with the hours he was working and his general disinterest in getting Gus to the vet in the first place.

Abbie's hand came to rest on his arm, and she stepped closer to him. The intoxicating scent of her honey shampoo hit him then. "I can help take care of him. Gus can stay with me if it comes to that."

He met her eyes and lost himself in such gentle compassion. This woman was always meant to be his wife. He stole a look at her bare left hand and frowned. What would it take to make her see they could work this out?

"We'll figure it out," he finally said to the doctor.

"Between the two of us, we can work something out."

He could finish out the season, traveling to as many events as it took to draw Tornado and hopefully win that title before the bull was retired at the end of the year. If he was ending this chapter of his life, he wanted to leave it on a high note. His dad would be prouder of him taking that shot at the title rather than quitting earlier since he was so close.

"Due to his age, Gus needs someone to keep a close eye on him overnight to ensure he doesn't have any negative reactions to the medication," Dr. Charles added.

Abbie could come to watch him compete at some events, and be waiting for him at home when others concluded.

"No problem," Abbie answered. "I'll watch him."

Tonight was round one, and he'd been counting on Abbie to attend the event with him. Didn't even care if the media snapped some pictures of the two of them. But without an interview as leverage and Gus requiring constant attention, he was out of ideas. "Are you sure, Abbs?"

"Of course." She wouldn't meet his eyes though, and that alone was cause for concern. "Your grandpa doesn't have the time, and Cliff and Erin won't mind a second dog in the guest cottage if it's for a good cause."

"I guess it's settled, then," he said. "Can we see Gus now?"

———

Gibbs didn't quite know what to make of the new house guest. Logan watched him pace around the couch a couple of times, undoubtedly wondering why another dog was in his off-limits spot. "You sure you don't mind Gus on the couch? He's kind of an outdoor dog." *Dirty and dusty.*

"He's fine. There're plenty of old blankets down."

Gus was livelier than he'd been since Logan first saw him, but the medication added a layer of drowsiness. He sat along the edge of the couch, gently stroking his dog as Gus dozed in and out of sleep. He'd listened to the dreaded voicemail as Abbie drove them back to her cottage, but Grandpa didn't have much to say other than he had no intention of paying for some expensive surgery. But his voice cracked near the end, leaving Logan to believe his grandpa cared a great deal about the dog.

Grandpa had tried to remove the tick. Probably thought he got the whole thing, too. He didn't look forward to telling him the botched result of his good intentions, but it'd have to wait yet again because when he returned his call, he found the voicemail box still full.

"I know you're riding tonight"—a hand dropped on his shoulder and he let his gaze travel to those chocolatey eyes—"but someone has to watch Gus. It can't be you, so it has to be me." Neither needed to mention Grandpa, who'd be working a late shift at the cement factory. Though Gerald hadn't been forthcoming about his two-job schedule, Abbie had managed to ferret out the details through connections she'd made.

Despite his disappointment, he felt hopeful too. They seemed to be working as a team again. He'd missed this more than anything, how effortlessly they worked together. "I was thinking, Abbs."

"Never a good sign." A twinkle danced in her eyes, and she sat beside him nice and close. She wrapped her arms around his free one, her head resting on his shoulder. Her honey shampoo blanketed him in an aromatic cloud. "Fire away."

"Why don't you finish that interview?"

She didn't say anything right away. Seemed she had to process his words first. "Why? I'm not going to ask Vince to give me my job back. Everyone seems to think he'll beg me to come back, but you don't know my uncle. He's stubborn. Prideful. Some days I think he'd rather let the paper sink than try anyone else's idea that might help it thrive."

"All valid points." He wriggled his arm free and wrapped it around her shoulders, drawing her close enough for a tender kiss that left them both a little breathless. "This interview might give you options, though. The most I do is talk for a few seconds to the camera crews that follow us around. I dodge all the personal, more in-depth questions."

"Your sponsors must hate that."

"They're not fans, but they certainly like it when I win." He laughed. "Might be worth something.

You'll have material I haven't shared with anyone else."

"You think I should write it anyway?"

"I do."

She pulled her head back and looked him over with a raised eyebrow. "And you'll cooperate?"

"Yes."

"In exchange for?"

He shook his head. "Nothing."

"You're not going to insist I come to the rodeo or go on another canoe ride in the moonlight?"

He chuckled. "You almost sound disappointed."

"Hardly." But that cute smirk she sent him over her shoulder when she went in search of her notepad said otherwise.

bbie

"Why are we attempting to move this dresser?" Erin demanded after their third failed attempt to shove the heavy piece of furniture more than an inch. "Or should I call it a giant boulder?" The bulky thing had been in that bedroom ever since Abbie could remember. She understood why no one had been eager to move it out when she moved in.

She didn't want to tell Erin the truth, but she'd had no luck getting her brother over to help. And asking Logan was out of the question. He'd already left for the arena anyway. "I dropped something. It's wedged down there."

"Why didn't you get your muscly cowboy to help you when he was here earlier?"

"We were busy."

"Abbie!" Erin scolded.

"I didn't mean *that*! He was helping me finish the interview." She wedged herself back in the corner, her back flat against the side of the dresser and one foot propped against its side, ready to push. "One more time."

"Okay, I'm lost."

The dresser didn't budge. "Were you even doing anything?" She looked over her shoulder at her idle friend.

Erin's hands were on her hips. "Why are you writing that article? Did I miss something? Seriously, I can't keep up with you two! If I'm not careful, you'll be hitched and I'll have missed the wedding."

Heat rushed to her cheeks, and she ducked back in her corner. "C'mon, help me out here." Probably *not* the time to mention what the item she sought was, the very engagement ring Logan gave her at Shimmering Lake that moonlit night so long ago. It might give Erin premature ideas. Abbie was only beginning to think she might have a future with Logan again, but her fortified walls had yet to completely crumble away.

Another hearty push from them both resulted in the dresser shifting almost two inches, enough for Abbie to stick her arm behind and wedge it underneath. Her fingertips brushed the ring. Another inch or two and she'd be able to grab it.

"He seems serious, Abbs."

"Got it!" With the ring tucked securely in her clenched palm, she wriggled free of the claustrophobic corner. She'd ask Logan to help her move the monstrosity back tomorrow morning when he came by to check on Gus.

"*What* exactly?"

If she thought she had a half-decent chance hiding the ring from Erin, she might've tried. Instead, she unfolded her fingers and held out her hand.

"Is this . . .?"

"Yep."

"You kept it. You told me you pawned it."

"I did." She dropped onto the edge of the bed. Gibbs gave her a side glance then tried to discreetly climb up behind her. The mattress sank instantly, but she didn't fall back because he curled up behind her, head poking out around her hip.

Erin stated the obvious. "You bought it back."

"The next day." That little decision had cost her a pretty premium. Needless to say, she refused to have anything to do with that little shop's ad fee collection. If it had been up to her, she wouldn't have sold them ad space in the *Starlight Gazette* to begin with.

Erin sat next to her, but Gibbs wedged his giant

head between them. "You've never really stopped loving him, have you?"

Abbie held the ring tightly between her fingers, considering putting it back on if only to prevent it from falling into the floor vent next. She couldn't fathom the task such a disaster would create in retrieving it from the duct work. "No."

"But you said—"

"I've followed every event. Watched every snippet of video interview I could find . . . except the rides themselves."

"You're really not going tonight?"

"Someone needs to keep an eye on Gus."

"I can."

The air suddenly felt stuffy, her throat tight. "I can't do it, Erin. I can't watch him ride another bull. I-I . . . Did you know I actually went to Vegas to watch him last year?"

"You said you were going for a story!"

"As soon as I sat in the stands and the first rider came out of the chutes, I lost it." It was miserable, sitting there sobbing uncontrollably as the people around her gave her odd looks and asked if she needed to call someone to come get her. It'd been nearly impossible to escape that crowd and run, but she managed. "I always see that bull trampling him. Tossing him around like a rag doll."

She hadn't realized tears were dropping until one splashed the back of her hand. Gibbs licked her arm and rested his head in her lap. He knew he wasn't allowed on the bed, mostly because she didn't have enough room to stretch out if he shared the space, but her need for comfort negated the rules.

"You'll never have the closure you need if you can't face this fear, Abbs."

"I just . . . I don't think I can."

"He's ridden for the last two years without serious injury, right?"

"Just a sprained wrist and a dislocated shoulder." It was crazy to think of those injuries as minor, but with a bull rider, it was never a matter of *if* they would get hurt. It was always a matter of *when*. Always sending up a prayer that when that happened, they could recover from those injuries.

"You have to go tonight."

Her hands trembled as they combed through Gibbs's soft ears. "I can't do it alone."

"Your mom is taking Izzy. Go with them."

Her objections overcome, she feared she no longer had a choice. "Okay."

"First, we need to get you cleaned up a bit." Erin looked her over, unimpressed with her cotton T-shirt and lack of makeup.

"Is that really necessary?"

Erin pulled her up by her wrists and hauled her into the bathroom, a devious twinkle in her eyes. "Absolutely."

———

The hum of music and a talkative crowd waiting for the event to start sifted through the air. Abbie's mom looked her up and down as they made their way from the overcrowded parking lot to the VIP stands. "You're a little dolled up tonight," she said. "Anything I should know?"

"Blame your daughter-in-law."

"Honey, you looking *stunning*." The sparkle in those eyes said Mom meant it, too. "Doesn't she, Izzy?"

"Yeah, stunning!" Izzy said with a bashful blush, hugging her grandma's arm a little tighter for a moment. "Is Aunty Abbie going to marry Logan?"

That question again.

"I don't know, sweetie," the older woman said in answer. "Guess we'll just have to wait and see."

Luckily, Abbie's long, curled hair was down and able to hide her reddening cheeks. She'd worn the ring, much against her better judgment. A part of her wanted to see whether Logan would notice. How he'd react. The other part of her simply tried it on and hadn't been able to get it off.

"I can get some shortening from the kitchen." Erin studied said finger and said, "Worked like a charm the last time that happened to me."

But Abbie turned down the offer, a little hopeful part inside her wanting to believe the luck was really fate. Plus, fidgeting with a ring that didn't want to slip off helped her distract herself from the fears tumbling in her stomach. Without the distraction, she might not be able to fight the urge to run far away from the arena.

Now she shoved her left hand in a back pocket of her shorts to avoid her mom noticing. She wasn't ready for the string of questions that might follow, or worse, the interrogation she might get once her mom shared that detail with her dad.

After collecting some hot dogs—Izzy's requested new favorite—they found their seats. Though the show hadn't officially started, the clown called out to the crowd, asking where everyone was from.

"What's he standing on?" Izzy asked.

"It's called a shark cage." Abbie pointed to the round contraption in the center of the ring. The top was a flat slab, the sides metal bars. "There're people inside with cameras." She tried to keep her voice even, but a memory of a bull charging right at a shark cage and nearly knocking it over flashed through her mind.

Her mom squeezed her shoulder. "You can do this, Abbs."

Able to offer only a weak smile, she concentrated on steadying her breathing. It would be mortifying to have a meltdown before a single rider had taken the field. "Erin talk to you?"

"A little."

"Do you think I'm making a mistake?"

"It doesn't matter what I think, does it?" Her mom gave her a comforting smile. "But I did hear something a little alarming."

"Oh?"

"Honey, you *quit*?"

"Maybe it was the wrong thing to do," she said, "but it felt right. I can't explain it." She traced the wood grain of the table in front of her. "I wish Grandma were still here. She'd let me print the stories I wanted. At least let me try a couple to see if they were successful. Vince won't even consider it."

"He's had a tough life, Abbs."

She'd heard it before, and some of it was true. He'd lost his wife to an aggressive cancer five years ago. His only kid stopped talking to him almost completely after that and moved halfway across the world. The paper was all Vince had left of family. "I only wish he could see what he's doing. I know the paper is important to him, but his pride gets in the way."

"Yes, it does."

"Do you think he'll come around? Everyone else seems to think he will."

"I think you know better."

Sadly, she had feared that all along. She didn't know what to do about her dream of someday running the *Starlight Gazette*. Vince liked to hold grudges, and he might very well hold one over her indefinitely. Sell the paper upon his retirement rather than keep it in the family as Grandma had wanted.

The main announcer asked everyone to stand for the playing of the national anthem. *This is it.* Any thoughts about running would need to be carried out or put to bed. If she had come alone, she definitely would've fled. But Izzy reached for her hand as a young woman sang a beautiful rendition of "The Star Spangled Banner," and it kept Abbie rooted in place.

At the conclusion, the announcer made dramatic introductions of all the riders, giant pictures backlit by flames displayed on the big screens, along with the rider's name, rank, and hometown.

It shouldn't surprise her that some of the names she became familiar with throughout Logan's career were among those introduced tonight. They were some of the best in the world, Logan among them. But he'd never compared himself to anyone else. It was something she admired.

"Out in the arena, none of that matters," he told her once, in a canoe on Shimmering Lake, if she recalled right. Or maybe all the best memories rewrote themselves to be played out at their favorite moonlit lake. "In the arena, it's only you and that bull."

"What goes through your mind when that gate

opens?" she'd asked him earlier today for her interview.

His answer was accompanied by a sneaky kiss to her neck. "Just hang on. It's only eight seconds; keep it simple."

Simple. How could any tangle with an eighteen-hundred-pound bucking bull be simple?

Her palms grew sweaty when Logan's named blared from the speakers. A favorite classic rock song played at his introduction, the same song they'd play when the gate opened and he shot out of the chute on a fierce bull. A *bull.*

"That's Logan!" Izzy pointed to the big screen. "Number one!"

"That's right, he's ranked number one," Mom said. And thankfully so. Abbie wasn't sure she was capable of actual words until the event concluded. "That means he's the best."

Logan scanned the crowd, but the sun shone into the eyes of the lined-up riders; it didn't seem he'd spotted her in the stands.

The years they spent together flashed through her mind. He had been prepping to be a bull rider since he was old enough to walk. She went to rodeo after rodeo when they were teenagers, and though he suffered sprained and broke bones and once even punctured a lung, never once was she afraid he'd be hurt beyond fixing.

"Don't think about it, Abbs," Mom said. "It won't do any good."

It was too late. Her mind raced with her worst fears. It would take all her willpower not to leave the arena. But she couldn't stay in her seat. She jumped up. "Who wants ice cream?"

"Meeeee!" Izzy cried instantly.

"I'll be right back with some." She practically ran before Izzy asked to come with her.

*ogan*

Logan walked along the bullpens in the back holding area, stopping to lean on a fence railing. He searched for the black and white spotted bull that had changed the entire course of his life. *Tornado*. He repeated the ritual every event, but what he hoped to gain, he couldn't quite say.

He was prepared to ride Tornado tonight, but the draw said otherwise. He'd been ready for months, and that almost made it worse. Made him antsy for something outside his control. No other bull fazed him, but Tornado wasn't just another bull.

He'd been waiting for three years—one spent

broken and healing, two competing—to beat the bull that nearly killed him. Tornado robbed him of his life, turning everything upside down after that ugly ride.

Knowing Abbie still cared about him made him feel invincible. He didn't doubt he could ride eight seconds tonight, not at all. If he could face the bull this weekend, maybe he'd recoup most of what he lost.

"Chase got him," one of the other bull riders, Cole, said to him, joining him at the fence.

Tornado had been known to hurt more than a few riders bad enough to hospitalize them. It was a miracle he hadn't killed any of them. "Wish I could trade him," he responded. Chase was a young kid, with a young family. A lot to risk for such a fierce bull.

Logan had drawn Storm Warning, a good bull that liked to spin. He'd scored well the two different times he drew him before. But it wasn't Tornado.

"There's still tomorrow."

"True enough." They chatted a few minutes about the muddy arena, the bulls, Cole's family back in Arkansas. Then Cole excused himself, leaving him alone once again outside the pen of bulls. Tornado turned his head in his direction. The familiar, crazy glimmer filled those untamed eyes.

"Why is Tornado such a tough bull?" Abbie had asked during their earlier interview session. He had to hand it to her, she kept her emotions in check. Especially since she tried to get Tornado stricken from the association after Logan was hospitalized. But the bull would have to do a whole lot worse to be removed from the roster before his planned retirement date.

"He averages a ninety-percent or better buck-off rate every season, for one," he answered, and waited for her to jot down some notes about it. "No matter how few or how many rides he has, most never last more than two seconds."

"So, to draw him is to basically accept you're not going to score?"

"No one ever accepts that they'll be bucked off, but I think with Tornado the nagging fear is a little more prominent. And if you get bucked off, you gotta run. Tornado has a bad habit of chasing his riders to exact his revenge."

He wished Abbie was here tonight to watch him, like old times. Though bull riding would always be a part of who he was no matter what life had in store for him, it felt more special when she was a part of it all. But he'd be devastated if anything happened to Gus in their absence.

He pushed away from the fence, his gaze lingering on Tornado as he walked away.

Judith and Izzy were supposed to come watch him tonight. He searched the crowd earlier, but the sun had been glaring right in his eyes when he attempted to find them in the VIP section. Since his ride was the second to last of tonight's round, he decided now was as good a time as any to say hello.

He weaved his way through the crowd, keeping a brisk pace and avoiding eye contact with anyone who turned his way. The fans were part of the package deal, but tonight, he couldn't handle the extra attention. Luckily, most of the media hadn't been allowed in the VIP section tonight. Tomorrow, they were expected to be crawling everywhere. A feeling of what he suspected was relief coursed through him at the thought of retiring and settling down.

That's new.

Absorbed in his thoughts, he missed the girl in his path until he plowed right into her. Ice cream cones went flying, one narrowly missing a little boy. "I'm so sor—Abbs?" He had to step back and do a double take, because Abbie was . . . well, she was absolutely beautiful. She'd not only shown up, but obviously went through a bit of trouble to do so.

She stood there, arms raised, hands empty. "I know you like ice cream, but I didn't think you'd be so upset at being left out."

He laughed, that easy, unguarded laughter that made his tense muscles instantly unwind. "I'll buy new cones. Guess Izzy won't be too happy if you return without them."

He reached for her hand without thinking, because it seemed the most natural thing to do. He held his breath until it felt as if she didn't plan to wriggle free. Instead, she used their joined hands to pull him toward the ice cream concession. "Erin's watching Gus tonight," she told him.

Yeah, retirement has a nice little ring to it.

He felt something there, on her hand. Her *left* hand. At the window, as she ordered replacements, he lifted her hand into view and turned it over. "You kept it." His words were hardly a gasped whisper as shock swept over his body. It was *the* ring.

"I did."

"Does this mean—?"

"That'll be eight dollars," the concession worker said. Abbie looked expectantly at him.

"Oh, right."

"You *did* knock them out of my hand," Abbie said. "It's only fair."

He reluctantly let go of her hand and dug his wallet out of his back pocket to pay for the now four cones. How she had been carrying three before was a mystery to him. The things were enormous.

"You sure you want to eat this before your ride?" Abbie asked.

It was touching that she remembered how eating before a ride usually made him quite ill. But over the last two years, he'd worked his way through that hurdle. "I'll save the victory dinner for *after*, but a little ice cream cone won't do me in."

"Little? That thing is as big around as my arm."

He smirked, then bopped her on the nose with the tip of his cone, successfully leaving a blop of vanilla behind. The fire in her eyes warned him she might try to get even, but she pulled back just in time.

"You're lucky you're wearing your riding clothes." She shuffled both her cones to one hand and grabbed a napkin for the ice cream spot. "Otherwise, I'd make you wear one of these cones."

He wanted to put his arm around her as they laughed, but with a cone in each hand, it didn't seem wise. "You look beautiful tonight, Abbs. Really amazing." She rewarded him with a blushing smile. "The ring, that's what you lost behind the dresser, wasn't it?"

She worked at her cone and answered with a simple nod. He wasn't sure what it all meant, but since she'd gone through an awful lot of trouble to get to it and wore it now, he felt optimistic.

He'd been thinking about their future nonstop since that kiss in the back yard yesterday. Truth be told, he'd never really stopped thinking about it. But now it was the loudest thought stuck on a replay loop. He'd kissed Abbie many times, but this kiss was different. It spun his entire world upside down and sideways. It felt like forever. Like home.

Sunday, after Izzy's birthday party was over, he'd tell her about the house. He planned to drive her over there with a blindfold and surprise her. He originally thought he'd put it in her name, let her sign all the closing paperwork, so it was completely her own. But now he wondered if they couldn't buy it *together*. "I could've helped you move that dresser, you know."

"I managed." They'd reached the stands, and Izzy caught sight of him with a squeal of excitement.

"When's it your turn, Uncle Logan?" Izzy asked Logan.

Uncle? The title warmed a spot inside his chest. He'd not only missed Abbie; he'd missed being a part of this family.

The first couple riders had already taken their turn. Interesting that Abbie chose the very beginning of the event to track down treats for the group. Her back was turned toward the arena now as they announced the next rider and prepared to open the gate. "I'm one of the last guys to go tonight, so it'll be a while."

"Is it hard?" Izzy's innocent blue eyes watched the rider for the four-point-eight seconds he lasted.

"Harder than staying on a sheep, that's for sure," Judith said.

"Skittles didn't spin around in circles." Wise words for such a young, observant girl. "And she didn't have horns. Do they hurt?"

Though he was enjoying the questions from such an inquisitive little mind, Abbie seemed a little pale over it. He suspected she'd remain that way until he finished his ride and proved everything would be just fine. "They can hurt, yes. Quite a bit."

Izzy licked vigorously at her ice cream once her grandma pointed out it was melting fast, but her eyes shot back to the arena each time a rider came out of the chute. He wondered what other thoughts were going through her brilliant mind. He predicted she'd do quite well if she wanted a rodeo career someday.

"Vince tried to call me," Abbie said nonchalantly. As though she might've just mentioned the partly cloudy weather forecast rather than the former boss who crushed her most sacred dream.

"Did he?"

"Left a voicemail," she admitted, but quietly enough that her mom didn't hear. "I haven't listened to it yet."

"Maybe he came around."

"Doubtful."

He wanted to question it, but left it alone. She hadn't talked at all about what she would do now. As far as he knew, she wasn't even browsing online jobsites. He wished there was something he could do to fix it. "You should still see what he has to say. People can surprise you sometimes."

"I'll listen to that voicemail after you talk to your grandpa."

"Fair enough."

They watched the riders, or least everyone did but Abbie, who did a pretty good job of keeping her nose buried in her phone. Izzy buzzed with questions too smart for a five-year-old until it was time for him to return to the chutes and prepare for his first ride of the event.

He squeezed Abbie's hand, hoping to discreetly pull her attention from her phone for a few seconds. He admired the ring that still looked so perfect on that finger until she finally looked up at him. "It's going to be okay, sweetheart. I promise."

"You can't promise anything, Logan. You know that." She tried to smile, but the worry in her eyes dissolved it. "Just be careful, okay?"

He brushed his hand along her cheek, bringing her lips to his own. He didn't care if Izzy or her mom were watching. Or the crowd. No need to keep it a secret. They would make this work. He would stop at nothing to make sure of it.

———

Abbie

"*Tornado!*"

Abbie couldn't breathe at the loudspeaker's announcement. Seemed the universe was set on torturing her. She wished that of all the bulls, this one had been left behind for this particular rodeo. The only thing worse than having to watch a rider on that bull was to watch Logan on him again.

"You okay, Abbs?" Mom asked.

She'd forced herself to tuck away her phone and watch this one. Erin was right. She'd never have the closure she needed if she couldn't face her greatest fear. "I'll be happy when this is over."

With the chutes directly across from the VIP seating, she had much too clear a view of the black and white spotted bull and the rider maneuvering to find his balance behind the gate. Several bodies hovered around that small pen, trying to get Tornado under control. Until the rider was ready and gave the nod, they wouldn't open that gate.

"You used to love it, you know."

"That was a long time ago." Before she spent weeks in and out of hospitals with Logan. He'd been injured plenty through his many years of bull riding, but never like that. She feared she'd have nightmares about it the rest of her life.

"I remember you running into the kitchen when I was cooking dinner to tell me how he did," Mom said. "At least, for the rodeos I wouldn't let you travel to. You had such excitement in your eyes."

"I was young then. Naïve."

"You were supportive."

The debate paused as the gate flew open and Tornado shot out, bucking the second he was free. The bull rocked quickly, violently. The rider went flying early, and Tornado charged right at him before his feet even hit the ground, mud churning. If ever there was a bull that held a grudge, it was this one.

One-point-seven seconds.

The bull fighters made quick work of distracting Tornado, but he powered through them. Knocked one down and stepped on a shoulder in his destructive path. Abbie felt like throwing up.

The rider had one leg over the fence railing when Tornado reached him. The pickup man on his horse lassoed the bull and fought to pull him away, but not before Tornado got in a good, hard jab. The rider fell backward, his cry of pain heard across the arena, the crowd stunned into silence.

Her fingers clenched the seat beneath her until Tornado reluctantly allowed himself to be ushered out of the arena. He tried to turn around before the gate was latched, but wasn't quick enough to escape. She wanted to run. The thought of staying to watch even one more rider made her queasy.

But there were only two left.

"That's Logan!" Izzy happy-shouted, pointing to the big screen, seemingly unaffected by the horror she just witnessed. Or perhaps several minutes had lapsed since she had been able to hear anything outside the pounding of her own heart. "He's next, Aunty Abbie!"

"Storm Warning," her mom read off the board. "I

want a job naming the bulls. I think I'd be pretty good at that, don't you think so, Izzy?"

"You could name one Skittles!"

"Or Tsunami," Mom suggested.

The two came up with an entire slew of names, but Abbie didn't hear much of it. Her eyes were locked on Logan in the chute, dropping onto the bull. Storm Warning didn't give him near as much grief as Tornado had the previous rider.

The gate opened, and quickly the nauseated feeling gave way to a hint of excitement. She found herself at the edge of her seat as the bull bucked and kicked up mud. Logan held on. He moved in sync with the bucking as easily as breathing, rocking forward when the bull reared onto his hind legs. Backward when Storm Warning dropped onto all fours.

He'd improved his technique since she'd last watched him. Everything was smoother.

Each movement seemed to play out in slow motion until the buzzer sounded and Logan jumped off the bull, running for the gate.

"He did it!" Izzy cheered.

"He sure did, Peanut!" For the first time in years, Abbie felt a sense of relief. Logan wasn't ranked number one for nothing. He was born to do this, and from the smile on his face in the arena as he awaited his score, she knew he loved it. The familiar thrill she used to feel pulsed through her, and she wasn't quite sure how to feel about that.

"Eighty-eight points!" Her mom clapped her hands.

"Is that good?" Izzy asked.

"It's really good."

She could never ask him to give this up before he was ready. This was his passion. If she wanted them to work, she had to accept it.

While they waited on the final rider, the announcer provided the crowd with an update on Chase Wilder, the rider beat up by Tornado, as well as the bull fighter who was stepped on. "We're happy to tell you folks that both men will be okay." The crowd cheered, but Abbie waited for the *but*.

"It is believed that our fearless bull fighter has a broken shoulder and sprained ankle. Chase Wilder has a couple cracked ribs they think, but both are expected to make a full recovery."

The excitement she felt only moments ago deflated with a pop. How could the announcers possibly promise the crowd the men would recover so easily? They said the same thing about Logan before the ambulance hauled him away.

ogan

Parking his truck in his grandpa's driveway, Logan braced himself for battle. They'd been playing a passive-aggressive game of phone tag all week, but he was tired of it. At one time, he and his grandpa were close. What he knew about cars, which admittedly was a whole lot less than he knew about riding bulls, he'd learned from Grandpa.

He saw that the yard had been revived and tamed. The grass was cut, weeds gone, fresh mulch down. Flowers that'd been suffocating and invisible on Monday now had room to breathe and blossom.

"What's this?" Grandpa stomped onto the porch,

waving a folded piece of paper at Logan before he even had a chance to close his truck door. "I told you I didn't want your money. And where's Gus?"

"Gus is fine. He's with Abbie."

"What right did you have?" He shoved the papers at Logan's chest. Ah, so it was the notice from the bank for settling the debt.

He could shout right back, raise his voice about how he only ever meant to help, but arguing would get them nowhere. It never had. He nodded to the chairs on the front porch and took a seat in one himself. "You're the reason I know how to change my own oil, Grandpa."

The stern expression didn't soften any, but his grandpa did sit. "Can't imagine you have time for something as mundane as changing your own oil."

He had plenty of time between events the last couple of years, when he found himself home alone in Albany instead of in Starlight with his family and friends. "I do most of them."

This tidbit seemed to surprise Grandpa. Why hadn't he started things out this way when he came by earlier this week?

"You've done so much over the years for me and Mom," he continued now that he seemed to have Grandpa's unbiased attention. "I know I'm not around like I used to be to help out. I'm going to change that," he said. "Bought a house, actually."

Grandpa grunted, giving a curious glance as his

shoulders momentarily unclenched. "You're done riding, then?"

"I will be, at the end of the season."

The hard frown returned. "No, you won't."

The temptation to ride would always tug at him, he knew. But once Tornado was retired, there didn't seem a point to keep at it. He'd made more money than most bull riders his age, enough to retire if he wanted. He'd loved every minute of his career, but he wasn't too fond of traveling without Abbie. He wanted them to build a life together, and it helped a whole lot if he was around to do that.

She surprised him last night. He was certain she'd freak at him up on a bull and sprint out of the arena before he could get to the buzzer. He remembered the terrified look in her eyes while he laid almost immobile in a hospital bed for weeks, more broken bones than anyone cared to count.

"I'm going to marry Abbie."

"You've said that before."

"I mean it this time."

Something almost resembling a smile tried to settle on those straight lips. "She's okay with you still riding out the season?"

"She's not crazy about it, but she understands." She *had* been truly excited for him last night. The moment she saw him approaching the stands, she ran into his arms and kissed him in front of everyone, including the flashing cameras allowed into the VIP section at the conclusion of the round. "I want to open a bull-riding school."

Grandpa scoffed at that idea. "What you want to waste your money on that for?" But the harshness wasn't as heavy in his tone anymore.

"There'll always be bull riders, Grandpa. Might as well teach 'em what I know."

They sat in silence for a bit, the enjoyable kind that had been a myth between them for years. The barn could still use a fresh coat of paint, but Logan would help accomplish that himself.

"Gus has Lyme disease," he said several minutes later. "Doctor says he'll be okay. Just needs medication twice a day for an entire month. Abbie's been watching him. I know you don't really have that kind of time."

"I pulled a tick off him last week." Grandpa sat forward, a heavy sigh releasing. "Should've taken him to the vet and let them pull it out. I just . . ."

"No one's blaming you, you know."

"You can't just show up after being gone all this time and try to fix everything." Though firmness hummed from that tone, the harshness had faded, gone entirely now.

A glance at his phone warned him he was about out of time. He stood. "I wanted you to have options. You took us in when Mom lost the ranch." He didn't mention anything about the ranch being converted into a concrete factory. Grandpa obviously knew, and there was nothing anyone could have done to prevent that. Nothing anyone could do now. "I know money doesn't fix everything, but covering the bank loan was something I could *do*, so I did it."

"You didn't—"

"You can do whatever you want with the place. Keep it. Sell it. But at least now *you* get to decide, not the bank." He hopped off the porch. "There's still a seat for you at the rodeo tonight if you want it." But he didn't wait for his grandpa to tell him he had to work. They both knew he did.

———

Clouds hid the afternoon sun as Logan waited his turn to draw his poker chip. The riders, along with the bulls, were all assigned random numbers to determine the order the riders drew, and the bull they'd ride. Logan stepped up, reaching into a bucket to see what fate decided for him.

Twenty-three.

He had to double check the lineup to be sure, because after all this time it just didn't seem possible.

Tornado.

Handing his chip over so it could be officially recorded, Logan stepped off without saying a word to any other contestants. He needed some space, some quiet.

He took the long way to the VIP stands, slipping

behind as many concession buildings and tents as possible. Tonight, they had one set up for VIP guests to dine with the cowboys. But he needed a minute to compose himself before he returned to Abbie and her family.

After all this time, he finally drew the bull that had taunted him for three long years. He'd watched all the video footage there was of the bull. Every ride. He'd wanted to prepare himself for this day. Now his fears of never drawing the bull, never getting a chance to best him, were over.

He wished more than anything that his dad were here to offer him advice. If he got bucked off, he might not get another chance. He didn't always last eight seconds, but he did more than he didn't.

"There you are." Abbie reached for his hand, her warm smile smoothing some of his frayed nerves. "What's wrong?"

Part of him didn't want to admit the truth. Didn't want to give her anything to worry about the whole night until he rode. If he didn't mention drawing for his bull, she wouldn't know until the announcer told the crowd. It wasn't a secret he felt right withholding from her. "I drew him. I drew Tornado."

Her face paled. "Can you redraw?"

He squeezed her hand, and she squeezed back harder. "You know the rules. I either ride the bull I drew, or I don't ride."

"Then don't ride." Her voice quivered, eyes shiny with tears. "Please."

"Abbs, you know I have to do this."

She sucked in a breath, closed her eyes, and nodded. "I know. I just wish you didn't."

"One ride. That's it."

"What if you do it, Logan? What if you beat him?"

"Then I'll get to retire at the end of the season with a sense of accomplishment." A couple heads turned in their direction, and he pulled her back behind the concession buildings. The last thing he needed was word getting out about his retirement before he was ready to make the official announcement. His sponsors would have a hay day.

"Retire?" That single word brought a hopeful smile to her face. He wanted to share his plans for the two of them. Big plans. But he wasn't ready to spoil his surprise. Not yet.

"We'll talk more about it tomorrow, okay?" Drawing her into his arms, he kissed her until they were both breathless. Abbie was a little wobbly on her legs when they broke apart, so he wrapped her arm around his. "Suppose I better say hi to your family."

"Dad might come tonight."

His throat constricted, as though the air might have suddenly thickened and made it difficult to breathe. "That so?" The last image he had of Mr.

Bennington wasn't a pleasant one. The red face, the daggers in his eyes. The man swore he'd never forgive Logan for hurting his daughter.

"It'll be okay. You'll see."

The thought that the man might be sitting in the stands now made him more nervous than he ever was on a bull, but he didn't know how to avoid an inevitable encounter. Maybe he'd simply get lucky and Mr. Bennington wouldn't show.

"Logan!" Izzy ran right up to him and waited to be scooped into his arms. Before he could manage more than a couple words, a crowd gathered around. His friends, family, fans. "Are you coming to my birthday party tomorrow?"

"I sure am," he assured her.

"Promise?"

"Promise."

"Good!"

"Grandpa?" Logan was shocked to spot the older man in the tent, working on a barbeque rib. Even if he hadn't been scheduled to work tonight, their conversation this morning didn't seem near enough to mend their relationship. For his grandpa to show up to his event, even though he couldn't stand bull riding, had to mean they would be okay.

"Couldn't turn down the free food." Grandpa let out a deep, gravely laugh Logan hadn't heard in years. "Heard the new owner went all out on the catering. Did you know they got steak over there?"

Logan set Izzy down when she began wiggling and let her run back to her dad. The innocent little girl had no idea what was in store for her tomorrow. "I thought you had to work toinght."

"I quit." Grandpa tossed his cleaned rib bone into a nearby trashcan. "I'll be by to pick up Gus and his medication in the morning. He's my dog, too. I'll make sure he gets all the medication he needs."

Logan stared, a little dumbfounded. Seemed as if something was in the air lately. "You really quit?"

"Don't need that other job anymore. I got options." He clapped Logan on the shoulder, then excused himself to go in search of a steak dinner. It was the closest he'd get to a *thank you* from him, and that was okay. It was more than he expected.

———

Logan pushed away all thought as he prepared to drop onto the black and white spotted bull that was already agitated from the confines of the chute. The excitement of the crowd faded as though someone turned down a volume dial. Quieting his mind was the most crucial step of riding a bull. His dad taught him that.

Keep it simple. The countermovements to the bull and their timing were everything. If he focused on that, he might just last.

"Ready?" the flankman asked.

Logan nodded and dropped down onto the broad-backed bull. The chute, narrow for the bull's safety, kept Tornado from making any radical movements. It didn't stop him from trying, though. Logan fought to find his balance long enough to secure the rope around his right hand.

Tornado was never going to make a ride easy for him. If he did, Logan would feel cheated.

The bull jerked and kicked at the back of the chute. Everyone around him went into motion, ensuring both he and the bull were safe. The crowd noise filtered its way back; like radio interference, he forced it back out.

Keep it simple. When he felt as ready and balanced as he was going to be, he nodded.

The gate opened.

Logan's arm broke the plane of the chute, starting the clock.

Tornado jumped. Logan leaned forward at the hips, lifting himself, following the animal's momentum.

He anticipated the kick, transferred his balance to sit into it.

Tornado threw a spin into the next jump and he nearly flew off. His grip on his rope was fierce, though. He found a millisecond to right himself.

Aggravated that he had yet to buck the rider, Tornado picked up speed both with his jumps and his spins. The sporadic kicking jolted Logan. He felt himself slide.

The buzzer. Where is the buzzer?

He draped his leg over the bull. His hand remained wrapped in a rope he had to drop soon or risk a seriously hard fall . . . and severe injury.

He dug in his heel but was losing his grip.

The buzzer sounded. He dropped to the ground and rolled.

Tornado was quicker than any bull he'd ridden. Meaner. He was far from safe.

The image of Abbie at his hospital bedside, her eyes filled with terror of the unknown, propelled him forward in a dead sprint. He'd not let this bull send him back there. Not even for a scratch.

Feet from the fence, the bull's hot breath warmed the back of his neck.

He leaped, anticipating the blow to come. Praying for a sprain or something that only required stiches.

"And that's eight seconds, everybody!" the announcer shouted. The crowd screamed and cheered. "Give it up for your hometown rodeo star! Loooogaaaan Attwood!"

On the other side of the fence, he finally let himself look over his shoulder. Tornado had been roped by one of the pickup men. And though he fought it, the bull relented and went through the gate they opened for him.

He did it. He bested the beast.

"Eighty-nine points, ladies and gentlemen!" the announcer continued. "How fantastic is that? That puts Logan in first place."

The crowd erupted.

For three years, his life had been dictated by the bull that nearly cost him everything. The weight he'd carried lifted. The only thing he wanted to do now was run to the woman he loved and lift her into his arms to celebrate this victory together.

 bbie

Abbie'd held her breath so long she was having a hard time now that it was over. Standing was impossible with her uncooperative legs, so instead she leaned back in her seat.

Over. It was really over.

"He did it! He did it!" Izzy cheered. "Aunty Abbie, he did it!"

She scooped her niece into her lap and wrapped her in a hug. "He sure did, Peanut!"

Logan had drawn the bull that nearly killed him, and this time he beat him.

"That's the look I remember," her mom said.

It was true; she had forgotten how excited

she used to get when Logan had a good ride. Or any ride at all. Fear had only been a small, flaky thing all those years until the first serious injury. But since then, she'd let it control her. *Not anymore.*

Logan weaved his way through the crowd and into the stands to her. There were still a few riders left, so he slipped quickly into the vacant seat beside her to avoid blocking anyone's view. Izzy jumped into his lap before Abbie could throw her arms around him.

"You did it, Uncle Logan!" With Izzy still wrapped around him like a spider monkey, he managed to lean in for a kiss that left Abbie a little lightheaded. So many emotions packed into that kiss: exhilaration, relief, love.

"You *are* going to marry Aunty Abbie, aren't you?"

They both burst into laughter at Izzy's assessment. Logan cupped her jaw, his thumb brushing her cheek. "I sure hope so."

"Logan, that was incredible. What a ride." She went rigid at the sound of her uncle Vince's voice. Logan had mentioned something about the onslaught of media allowed in the VIP section tonight, but she assumed Vince would think twice about approaching Logan after the way the week had transpired.

"Thank you," Logan replied, keeping things

neutral, she noticed. For the benefit of everyone around them, no doubt.

"I was hoping you might answer a few questions for an old family friend." Vince tried that easygoing smile that sometimes worked, sometimes backfired. Her mom had been right, he'd had a hard life. Lost a lot of loved ones. She had stayed quite angry at him the past couple of days, but seeing him in person softened her ire.

"No interviews, please." Logan unwrapped Izzy and handed her to Abbie to pass down the line to her mother, who had a fresh bag of popcorn to share. "I'm just here to compete, nothing more."

Abbie bit back the urge to tell Vince she finished the interview. Didn't seem as though it mattered much now.

"I thought you might tell me a little about what it was like to ride Tornado. How you feel about it. How long you think it'll be before you draw him again."

Draw him again? Her stomach knotted at that dreadful thought. It was possible, she supposed. It'd taken him two years to draw him, but what was to say he wouldn't draw him once more? Twice more? He might draw him at his next event. What if that ride didn't go as smoothly?

"Maybe three questions so I have something to quote from you?" Vince tried again. "For an article about the rodeo."

"The only interview I consented to was the one

with Abbie. If you want to print it, you'll have to work that out with her." He kissed her on the cheek and hopped to his feet, leaving her with an enduring squeeze of her hand. She forced out all worries about him drawing that bull again. She couldn't stand to think about it. "If you'll excuse me, I have to head behind the chutes. They'll be announcing the results soon."

Vince seemed at a loss once Logan disappeared. He watched him go for a minute, but pride kept him from chasing after him. Or defeat. She wasn't quite sure which it was.

"Have a seat, Vince. You're family first." With the way he kept glancing around, it seemed he didn't want to take her up on her offer, but without an alternative, he finally sat.

"You finished it, then?" he asked, refusing to look anywhere but straight ahead as another rider prepared to exit the chute.

"Yes." There'd been so many things she wanted to say since the morning she quit, but a lot of them didn't seem important anymore. Vince would never set aside his pride to beg her to come back, and she wouldn't grovel.

"I'll make you a deal," she said. "I'll let you print my interview with Logan, but you're not allowed to edit a single word without my approval."

"Carl's working on our front-page story as we speak." Vince nodded across the stands where a meek Carl took notes. So the front-page replacement story was nothing more than rodeo results. Maybe a few play-by-plays of rides.

"Uncle Vince," she said, hoping the family endearment might soften his sharp edges long enough to really hear what she had to say. "My only dream since I was a little girl was to run the *Starlight Gazette* like Grandma used to. To write stories that gave people hope, that showed them how wonderful our community really is. We're not like other newspapers, and that's what I love the most about ours."

"Abbie—"

"I'll work with you on this"—she cut him off —"but this is a one-time offer."

For once, Vince didn't try to interject. He simply nodded at her and waited.

"I'll come back to work, but I have conditions. First, you will print this interview the way I wrote it."

He didn't seem too bothered by that if his expression, unchanged and blank, was any indication. Perhaps he trusted her a little more than he wanted to admit. "Fine."

"Second, you'll print the story about the Andersons' horse camp too. Next week's edition, not some time down the road. It's a wonderful program they have going, and our readers should know about it."

Vince removed his glasses and held them in his lap. Conflict swam in his eyes. "Done. What else?"

Good. He realized she wouldn't settle for only the easy items. "I want pages five through eight, and I want the freedom to publish whatever I choose. If the paper tanks because of it—which it won't, but if it does—I'll resign, and you can change things back to the way they are now."

"Four pages?"

By this point in the conversation, she caught on to her entire family eavesdropping from her peripherals. Seemed Vince realized it, too.

"And I want to write the front-page story every other week."

It had to be an uneasy feeling, relinquishing control of something he'd clutched so tightly for so long. But without her conditions, the paper would never be the way she dreamed. She couldn't work at the *Starlight Gazette* unless Vince was willing to give her the chance to at least try her ideas.

"Maybe I already have a replacement in mind for your spot," Vince said, but he couldn't meet her eye.

She patted his shoulder. "You don't or you wouldn't be entertaining my demands."

"You sure drive a hard bargain. I like your gusto. That's what you'll need to be successful in this industry, you know." He cracked a smirk. "Send me the story tomorrow night. Come back to the office Monday morning. Team meeting at nine-thirty."

Excitement ran through her veins, but she kept it contained. She wasn't trying to gloat in front of her boss, but it did feel as if everything was finally falling into place. Logan would retire at the end of the season, and they could finally start their life together. Plan a wedding, find a house.

At the last thought, she felt a little depressed. She wondered whose offer had been accepted and what they might do with the property. Her heart would shatter if a developer bought it to tear it down.

"And that was the last ride of the night, folks!" The announcer's voice roared through the crowd. "What a night! Let's get ready to congratulate our top-scoring riders."

Izzy crawled across a couple laps to arrive back in hers. "Did Uncle Logan win?" she asked, bright blue eyes filled with curiosity. Abbie loved that about the girl, and hoped one day soon to have her own son or daughter hungry for knowledge.

"They haven't announced it yet"—she rocked Izzy from side to side—"but we know he did because of his scores." She explained how they added together the scores from last night and tonight. "Highest total wins, and Logan had the best scores both nights."

"Does he get a trophy?"

"Maybe a belt buckle. But mostly, it's money," Vince chimed in. "And points."

Izzy seemed to process this information, surely a dozen more questions buzzing through her busy mind. But she settled on one. "Are there girl bull riders?"

"Some," Abbie answered, the question leaving her a little uneasy. "But not as many."

"Do you want to ride bulls, Izzy?" Vince's question was innocent enough, and no one else might've thought anything of it. But Abbie felt a little sick at the thought of her niece on a bull.

"I want to ride horses," Izzy finally said.

"You could be a barrel racer," Vince suggested. The conversation between the two continued, but she heard little of it. Suddenly, she wanted to be anywhere else as a horrid realization took root.

Bull riding was in Logan's blood. Something his dad and his dad's dad did because they had a calling. She thought she could survive the rest of one season with Logan riding. But how could she ever rest easy if a future son or daughter decided to follow the same career?

———

"Everything okay, Abbs?" Logan asked her that evening in the VIP tent, during the celebration the owner put on at the conclusion of the main event. "You seem a little off."

"Fine." But her smile was forced, and she was certain he could tell.

"I heard you got your job back."

No doubt her mom told him. Or Cliff. Her eyes danced back and forth between the two, trying to decide which it had been. Both had been more than interested in that little conversation.

"I did. On my terms."

"I'm proud of you, you know."

She kissed him then, hoping it would erase her earlier fears about their future children. It was a simple obstacle they could overcome together. *Right?*

The owner had opened the gates to the general public, and dozens of people wandered over, crowding the tent. She reached for Logan's hand, hoping to pull him from the chaos for a private moonlit walk. She had a lot of burning questions about their future.

They'd barely escaped the food tent when Logan was intercepted by Mrs. Hampton herself. Abbie couldn't find the words to say even a polite hello, because she was frozen on the woman who hadn't changed a bit in more than a decade. Same white hair kept in a bun, same high-necked blouse, same stern expression etched into the wrinkle lines on her face. The only thing missing was her broom.

"Mr. Attwood, a pleasure."

Logan shook her hand, as he had several others that evening. "Thanks for coming out, Mrs. Hampton."

"Please, call me Pearl."

Abbie, hand wrapped around his arm, felt it go

rigid. But his cool smile never faltered. "Hope you enjoyed yourself tonight."

"I did. My husband used to do some bronc riding back when he was younger. Brought back memories for sure."

"Good, I'm glad."

"That's why I'm selling, you know."

Abbie felt the air halt in her lungs. What an odd thing to say, because it wasn't directed at her at all but rather, at Logan. When had the two had the chance to talk about her house?

"I lost him last year. The house just feels too empty without him."

Her eyes bounced between Logan and the woman who'd chased her off her porch more than once. What was she missing? Because she was definitely missing something.

"I'm sorry for your loss."

"You'll take good care of it, won't you? That's why I chose your offer."

"*Your* offer?" Abbie dropped her hand and took a step away from Logan. Betrayal twisted inside her like a sharp knife.

"You didn't know?" Mrs. Hampton finally acknowledged Abbie's presence, her eyebrows drawn.

"The only thing I knew was that *my* offer didn't get accepted." Only the shock kept her tears at bay, but her flight instinct was as charged as ever. How could Logan have gone behind her back like this, and then kept such a big secret from her?

"I'm sorry, Ms. Bennington. You have to understand that house is worth a considerable bit more than you could afford. And with an offer like Mr. Attwood's, there was no way I could turn it down."

"Abbs—"

"Don't." Abbie tore her way through the crowd, refusing to look back until she reached her car. Her entire world seemed lopsided. Logan had held her in his arms and consoled her when she learned she hadn't gotten the house. But he'd known *he* got it all along.

The ring that before wouldn't budge now slipped off quite easily. She slammed it at the ground before she jumped in her car and drove away.

ogan

Despite his best efforts, Abbie refused to talk to Logan since she left last night. Mrs. Hampton couldn't have had worse timing. One day. Just one more day. That was all he needed to surprise her with the life ahead for them.

"You know Abbie doesn't like surprises," Erin said at breakfast the next morning as she passed the syrup for Izzy's requested chocolate chip pancakes— a meal Abbie didn't show up to share. His eyes kept falling on the cottage door, waiting to see it open and Gibbs burst through. The poor lug was missing out on some pretty good bacon.

"I know."

Cliff reached for his cup of coffee. "You remember the surprise birthday party out at the lake, right?"

He had once tried to throw Abbie a party, but she demanded he turn the car around before he could park near the crowd gathered under a picnic shelter. She hated being the last to know, no matter the reason.

"Aunty Abbie doesn't like surprises?" Izzy kicked at her chair, fork in one hand, her stuffed horse in the other.

"No, sweetie. Not so much," he answered.

"Then why'd you do it, Logan?" Erin asked. "Why did you think it was a good idea this time if it's never been before?"

"I couldn't tell her about the house when it all happened. She wasn't ready to hear it. You and I both knew she wouldn't get it with a letter, and if I didn't interfere, she'd lose the house for good." He filled his fork with the last bite of pancakes on his plate. "I have plans for our future. I'm retiring at the end of the season. Opening up a bull riding school."

"Pretty good idea," Cliff said.

Logan ruffled Izzy's hair, winning a giggle. "Thank this bright young lady here for planting the idea when we were at horse camp."

Erin sat back in her chair. "The house is for you *and* Abbie?"

"At first, it was just for her. I was going to put it in her name, let her sign all the paperwork. But things have changed since I made that decision. I want to share it with her. Build our life together there."

"She wasn't wearing her ring this morning." Erin's tone was grim, almost sympathetic. "I'm sorry to tell you, but you should know. It got stuck on her finger before, so she must've really wanted it off."

His heart dropped to the pit of his stomach. He pushed his pancakes with a fork while everyone ate in gloomy silence, surely unsure what else to say that could console the situation.

"You mind helping me with something after breakfast?" Cliff asked. He glanced at Izzy, and Logan knew not to ask questions.

His eyes landed on the cottage again, where there was movement in the living room window. Gibbs poked his head through an opening in the curtains. The urge to go over there and post himself outside until she answered the door tugged at him. But if he knew anything about his Abbs, it was that she needed time. Besides, he'd see her at Izzy's party. No way she'd miss that. "Sure thing."

———

Purple balloons lined the driveway and the columns of the front porch when Logan and Cliff returned to the house early that afternoon, horse trailer in tow. He couldn't wait to see the look on Izzy's face when she realized her parents bought her a horse for her birthday. A horse he helped Cliff buy without going into debt, but no one ever needed to know that detail.

Cliff typed a text, no doubt asking Erin for the signal.

He couldn't help but watch for Abbie, though he doubted she'd be in the front yard when the party was out back. "Want me to get her unloaded? Let her stretch her legs a minute before we take her back?"

"Yeah, that'd be great."

He busied himself with unloading the yet-to-be-named mare—that honor had to go to the birthday girl. The crunch of gravel beneath heavy tires and the roar of a diesel engine caused him to stiffen.

Mr. Bennington exited his duly truck and spotted him immediately. He'd been lucky to avoid him last night, especially after Mrs. Hampton made her appearance and unknowingly spoiled all he had worked to rebuild. The bulky man strode right over to Logan as soon as he saw him.

Reins in hand, Logan braced himself for whatever happened next. "Mr. Bennington." He reached out his hand, but didn't get the handshake he sought. Hadn't really expected to.

"I told you once before how I felt about you hurting my daughter." The man, a couple inches taller and definitely a few pounds heavier, pinned him with his stern eyes. "I won't let you do it again."

"I love your daughter."

"If you love her, you'll do what's best for her. That might mean leaving her alone."

Despite the hint to leave town and never return, because surely that was what Mr. Bennington wanted, he held steadfast. "I'll leave that up to Abbie."

"Buying her house behind her back, that was you leaving it up to her?"

He didn't think his intentions would matter much to Mr. Bennington. He was a man of action, not words. But before he could say anything more, they were interrupted.

"There you are!" Judith came around the side of the trailer, her eyes lighting up at the sight of the golden mare with the white mane. "Izzy's been asking about her grandpa for an hour now." She pulled on her husband's arm, dragging him away to the back yard. But not before giving Logan a wink over her shoulder.

What could that mean?

"We're on." Cliff took the reins from Logan and led the horse to the back yard.

The second Izzy laid eyes on the horse, she squealed. At the news that the horse was hers, she began to cry. "She's happy." Judith appeared beside him, nudging him. "Kids are funny creatures, you know? Emotional in unexpected ways. Something you'll want to keep in mind." She patted him on the arm and walked off toward the birthday girl and her new horse.

Hope bubbled inside him until he met Abbie's eyes and the scowl she sent his way. Obviously Judith and her daughter were on very different pages about him right now.

Gibbs watched from the window of the cottage, unhappy about his confinement. But if he'd never been around a horse before, it made sense not to risk spooking her. He sent the dog a little wave and eased his way through the family crowd until he was at Abbie's side.

"Abbs, can we talk?"

"No."

"The house, it was for *us*. For you."

She sucked in a breath before turning to face him. "You *lied* to me, Logan. I can't start a life with you based on a lie."

The words packed a worse punch than a hard hit from a bucking bull. The absence of her ring packed another. "*Lie?* It was a *surprise*, Abbs. Please, come with me to see the house. I want to tell you all about the plans I have. For us. For our future."

"Leave, Logan. Just please leave. I can't do this. I thought I could, but—"

"This isn't just about the house, is it?"

She glanced around him, but everyone seemed

preoccupied with Izzy and her new horse. The little girl was being hoisted into the saddle. He had only a moment to wonder how long it'd be until her feet reached the stirrups before Abbie answered him.

"What if our kids grow up and want to be bull riders, too?"

"I'm sure at least one of them will. Is that so bad?"

Tears of regret lingered in her eyes. "I can't do it, Logan. I can't."

His heart cracked open at those words. "Abbie, if you want me to go, I will. But I won't keep chasing you. If I leave this time, it's for good."

"I'm sorry." She briefly touched his arm. The remorse in those eyes would haunt him for years to come. Somehow he'd find the strength to figure out a life that didn't include Abbie Bennington. He'd always love her, but the fight in him was gone.

She'd broken his heart for the last time.

CHAPTER 22

Monday morning came too soon. Abbie hadn't slept well the night before; even Gibbs had been annoyed with her unusual amount of tossing and turning through the twilight hours. He'd abandoned the bed he wasn't allowed on for the off-limits couch.

She wasn't sure coffee could cure much right now, but she was on her third cup anyway.

Less than thirty minutes ago, she and Gibbs watched from the window as Logan drove away. Though they could hardly see more than the top of the truck cab, the dog whined as it left. Seemed he knew too—this time was different than the last. Gloomier.

Logan hadn't even said goodbye.

A glance at her bare left hand left her empty inside.

She wasn't ready to face anyone today, but she certainly couldn't call in sick after the way she confronted her uncle and finally made forward progress. Now was not the time to mess up any of that.

"Well, Gibbs, let's get to it."

"You all right, Abbs?" Mom asked, fishing out a peanut butter treat for Gibbs when they arrived at the store.

She wanted to be mad at Logan. Anger was the only thing that helped her hold it all together when he left the last time. "I'll be okay." He left without even an attempt to change her mind. No calls or texts either, no matter how many times she checked her phone. His words haunted her. *I won't keep chasing you.* Maybe this time, it really was too late to fix anything.

Gibbs leaned against her legs, licking her hand until she scratched his head behind his fluffy ears.

"Erin told me what he did."

"He lied to me, Mom."

"He *fibbed* about what he did *for you*, Abbs. Sounds like he had some big plans for you two, and you couldn't even give him the chance to share his vision with you." Her mom glanced at the front door as a customer entered. "You don't always have all the answers."

She couldn't talk about it anymore or she'd crack. Best thing to do, she reasoned, was to go to the office and lose herself in her work. She had four pages of next week's paper to plan, the blank slate she'd always wanted. She'd keep her head down and write every night until she couldn't keep her eyes open.

———

Throughout the week, Abbie threw herself into story after story. But today, she fought to maintain concentration. She was tired, and all the coffee in the world wouldn't save her. She'd conceived tons of story ideas over the last few months, but none seemed to grab her right now. Everything she typed up, she deleted.

Her phone buzzed on her desk, and her heart stopped. But it wasn't Logan.

Erin: Abbs, I love you. But you're an idiot.
Abbie: Gee, thanks.
Erin: Call him.
Abbie: He hasn't answered any of my texts :(
Erin: Then go.

Abbie: Where?
Erin: Wherever he's at this weekend. Get your butt on a plane ASAP!!!

She started a reply three different times, but deleted them all. Then she tried to text Logan again, but couldn't manage to find the right words for him either. Nothing she tried so far had worked, so why would new words matter? Calling him? No, she couldn't do that, even though everything inside her wanted him to come back.

Abbie: He didn't even say goodbye :(

She watched the little gray bubble on her phone, waiting for whatever Erin was typing to come through. After several seconds, her phone rang instead.

"Hey."

"Don't you *hey* me," Erin scolded. "Abbs, if you love him, why aren't you doing anything about it?"

She stood and moved to the door, slipping outside. She strolled down Main Street to avoid Jamie's eavesdropping. The girl was still completely starstruck over having met Logan after the rodeo last weekend. The mere mention of his name made her spew a dozen questions about him.

"What am I supposed to do, Erin?"

"Stop waiting for him to come back, for one. This pitiful woe-is-me thing you have going on is not your best look."

"But I—"

"Izzy, put that marker down!" Erin hollered. "I have to go. *Do* something about this, Abbs."

Hardly half a dozen moseyed steps down the sidewalk, another call came, but her hope dropped when she saw it wasn't Logan's name on the screen.

"Abbie?"

"Hey, Christy." Abbie waited, expecting the call to be about their next chocolate and *NCIS* marathon.

"Are you available next Thursday at nine?"

That seemed an odd time for their next hangout, but she could use a friend to commiserate with; Erin wasn't giving her any sympathy these days. "What did you have in mind?"

"You have an appointment at the title company to sign your closing docs."

"Come again?"

"Your house, Abbs. Logan bought it for you. He signed the addendum to put everything in your name. It's paid for, you just need to be there to sign the paperwork."

Her heart pounded in her ears at the news. He gave her the house. "You're sure?"

"Very. So, you'll be there to sign?"

She glanced down at her empty ring finger, panic clutching her chest. She'd tossed it away in the dirt parking lot like a fool. Could it still be there? "I'll call you back."

She hustled down the block to collect Gibbs early, determined to avoid her mom's prying questions. "I'll explain later." Gibbs barked all the way to the car and down Main Street, excited about whatever mysterious adventure they were embarking on.

Racing across town, she pulled in front of the gate to the arena parking lot. A metal beam blocked cars from entering, and forced her to park there. She and Gibbs crouched beneath the barrier and ran across the dirt lot. She tried to remember where her car had been Saturday night, but now in the daytime, it wasn't as clear as it'd been in the moonlight.

"Find it, Gibbs! Find my ring."

The dog went to town sniffing the ground, despite his complete lack of understanding what he was looking for. Likely he thought it was a treat or a squirrel of some kind.

She recognized a tree and hoped she wasn't wrong about its proximity to her parked car that night. The gloomy, overcast sky did little to reflect the ring's stone and give away its location. She dropped to her hands and knees, feeling the dirt in case it got buried.

"What are you doing, Abbs?"

Palms and knees in the dirt, she froze, staring at the shadow of a man in a cowboy hat hovering above her. "Cliff?" Slowly, she stood and dusted herself off. Her white capris were hopeless. "What are you doing here? I thought you were done with the security job." The last thing she would admit was that she threw her ring in a fit of anger and now it was quite possibly lost forever.

"I'm staying on a little longer." He reached into his pocket and held out a small object. "Looking for this?"

"You found it?" She practically tore it from his hands and slid it back on her ring finger. "Oh thank you, thank you!" She threw her arms around her brother and squeezed. "Where did you find it?"

"Someone turned it in with the lost and found. You're lucky they didn't pawn it."

"Have you talked to him?"

"He's pretty tore up about all this, Abbs."

Guilt clenched at her chest. She'd been so stupid to let Logan go, and now it might be too late. "I screwed up. Big time."

"Yeah, I think you did." Her brother gathered her into his arms and squeezed her tight. "What are you going to do to fix it?"

———————

Any other person might've called a guy before flying halfway across the country to join him. But Abbie hadn't been able to work up the courage. After receiving no responses to any of the couple dozen texts she'd sent him, the thought Logan might not take her call left her crippled.

Though she knew he'd never see her in the stands packed with a crowd this size, she stayed put through the entire event. The arena was twice the size as the one in Starlight, and Logan had never been the mingle-with-the-crowd type if he wasn't expecting someone. She watched him ride, but he was bucked off at four-point-six seconds.

Even the announcer said it didn't seem as if his head was in the game.

Unable to secure a VIP pass last minute, she waited by his truck. Without a score today, he'd duck out early, she had no doubt. She twisted the ring secured on her finger, searching for the confidence to say what she needed to.

"Abbie?"

"Hey." She felt like that shy teenager again, seeing Logan in a different light for the first time. They stood there, so much unsaid between them. She wanted to run to him, to pretend everything was just as it was before she ever knew he lied to her about the house.

"Why are you here?" He was cautious, guarded. She couldn't blame him. Her heart twisted. Loving a bull rider had never promised to be easy. Building a life with one harder yet.

"I was wrong, Logan."

They locked eyes for a moment, but he stepped away to load his riding gear into his truck. "You came all this way to say that?" He didn't sound amused or impressed. Just tired. Exhausted.

"I know why you bought the house."

"So?"

"And I know why you couldn't tell me."

Logan shut the back door of the truck now that everything was loaded. "Doesn't really matter now, does it?"

"I think it does." But her pleading didn't keep him from opening the driver's side door. He was going to leave, and there didn't seem to be much she could do to stop him.

"I meant what I said, Abbs. I'm done chasing you. The house is yours now, free and clear once you sign the paperwork."

She wedged herself between him and the truck before he could climb into the front seat. It was likely the last desperate attempt to change his mind she'd ever get. "I don't want it unless you're buying it with me."

"I can't do this, Abbs. I just can't."

She placed her hands on his shoulders and

forced him to look her in the eyes. "It was always meant to be *ours*. Since the first time Mrs. Hampton chased me away from the front porch with that broom and you were hiding behind that tree. It's always been our house, Logan."

"What are you saying?" The faintest hint of a smile appeared, the first sign of hope she'd seen in him tonight.

She reached her arms around his neck. "Marry me, Logan."

She waited for what felt like days for him to respond, holding her breath until his arms finally went around her, too. "Well, this is certainly an odd turn of events. You're serious?"

"I love you. I always will. I know life won't always be easy, and even if all our kids want to be bull riders, well"—she took a deep breath and let it out—"I'll have to accept it. You'll just have to hold me while I cry."

"*All* of them, huh?" He smirked at that and wrapped her a little tighter in his arms. The tension in his shoulders finally relaxed. "You really want to marry a bull rider?"

She held up her left hand, wiggling her ring finger for him to see. "Very much."

"Then I suppose we better head back to Starlight." He gave her a wink. "Hop in."

"Wait. There's one more thing before we go home."

Home. Her hands went to the back of his neck and pulled his lips down to hers. She kissed him with everything she had, as if it might be the last kiss they ever shared, though she hoped it would be the first of many, many more to come.

 **bbie**

One year later . . .

Abbie swayed on the porch swing, her feet tucked underneath her legs, a blanket in her lap as she edited the final words of an article. Gibbs snored at her feet. He'd only made one attempt to climb into the swing since they had it installed, but he hadn't cared a bit for the rocking motion.

Some days she still couldn't believe this big, beautiful Victorian house was her home.

Their home.

"Get it finished?" Logan stepped on the porch, the creak of wood under his boots alerting Gibbs. He lifted his head at Logan's approach and stretched lazily to his feet. The dog had doubled in size since they closed on the house.

"Just did." She closed her laptop and set it off to the side. Vince had given her free reign of half the paper, and it felt wonderful and freeing to write the kinds of stories that warmed her heart. The readership had responded positively to these stories, and begged for more. She'd also been learning more about the business side of things at the *Gazette*. The pace was slower than she cared for, but a compromise she was willing to tolerate since Vince had come around so far.

She waited for Logan to hurdle over Gibbs and join her on the swing. "How's it looking out there?" She nodded toward the new addition on the edge of the property. The large metal-sided barn would soon host its first weekend of bull riders. Twenty hopefuls signed up to learn everything they could from a retired champion.

"Everything's ready to go." He put his arm around her and pulled her closer. That intoxicating cologne would always make her a little dizzy. She hoped he never stopped wearing it. "I hope I'm making the right choice."

"You are." She kissed his cheek. "I believe in you, Logan. This is what you're meant to do. You're meant to teach other riders what you've learned. To help them be as safe as they can be when they're in the arena."

He tickled her under her chin and tipped her lips toward his. "So, you're not sorry you married me?"

She stole a kiss before answering. "Not sorry at all. I kinda love you, Logan Attwood." She flashed him a purposefully cheesy smile.

"Good, because I kinda love you, too, you know." He gently rubbed her rounded belly. "What if our little boy wants to be a bull rider? What then?"

"Then I'll be happy he has the world's best instructor on site."

~THE END~

The Starlight Cowboys series:

Cowboys & Starlight (Book 1)

Cowboys & Firelight (Book 2)

Cowboys & Sunrises (Book 3)

Cowboys & Moonlight (Book 4)

Cowboys & Mistletoe (Book 5)

Sign up for Jacqueline Winter's newsletter to receive alerts about current projects and new releases!

http://eepurl.com/du18iz

ACKNOWLEDGMENTS

To my critiquers: Nikki, Shanon, Barb, and Dorie. I cannot say enough how much I appreciate your flexibility and willingness to help with this story, despite my completely unconventional method :) This story is better for the feedback you provided, and I'm very thankful to have such a wonderful group at the ready!

To my editorial and production team: You guys are AMAZING! No one batted an eye when I confessed my plan to write books on this crazy timeline, and every one of you has come through for me. I'm such a lucky gal!

To Husker: Thank you for your patience and unconditional love. We have many walks to take to make up for the time you let me write.

To Andy: You have believed in me from the first day, and it means the world to me. When doubt creeped in, you helped shove it away. Thank you for being there every step of the way <3

ABOUT THE AUTHOR

Jacqueline Winters has been writing since she was nine when she'd sneak stacks of paper from her grandma's closet and fill them with adventure. She grew up in small-town Nebraska and spent a decade living in beautiful Alaska. She writes sweet contemporary romance and contemporary romantic suspense.

She's a sucker for happily ever after's, has a sweet tooth that can be sated with cupcakes, and believes sangria was possibly the best invention ever. On a relaxing evening, you can find her at her computer writing her next novel with her faithful dog poking his adorable head out from beneath her desk.